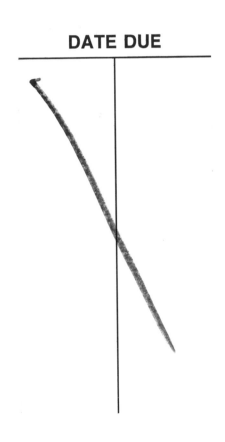

Original title: Tous les héros s'appellent Phénix
Written by Nastasia Rugani
© 2014 l'école des loisirs, Paris
English translation © 2016 Annick Press

Cover photography by Jock Sturges
Edited by Melanie Little
Proofread by Catherine Marjoribanks

Annick Press Ltd.

Cataloging in Publication

Rugani, Natasia
[Tous les héros s'appellent Phénix. English]
    About Phoenix / Natasia Rugani ; translated by Paula Ayer.

Translation of: Tous les héros s'appellent Phénix.
Issued in print and electronic formats.
ISBN 978-1-55451-842-5 (hardback).
—ISBN 978-1-55451-841-8 (paperback).
—ISBN 978-1-55451-843-2 (html).—ISBN 978-1-55451-844-9 (pdf)

    I. Ayer, Paula, translator II. Title. III. Title: Tous les héros s'appellent
Phénix. English.

PZ7.1.R84Ab 2016   j843'.92   C2016-900522-4
                             C2016-900523-2

Distributed in Canada by University of Toronto Press.

Published in the U.S.A. by Annick Press (U.S.) Ltd.

Distributed in the U.S.A. by Publishers Group West.

Printed in Canada

Visit us at: www.annickpress.com

Also available in e-book format. Please visit
www.annickpress.com/ebooks.html for more
details. Or scan

39905000762034

To my Pa2,

and to Stypo, my grandfather.

ONE

Darkness falls so quickly I don't have time to find the hole in the tire on my sister's bike. Lacking either a flashlight or a patch, we'll have to continue on foot all the way back to our house, about an hour and a half from the edge of the dark forest we're now in.

"I think a car's coming," says Sasha, crouching and pressing her ear to the ground.

I do the same, but all I can hear is some owls hooting.

"We're not getting in a stranger's car," I tell her.

"Even if it's Mike Archer?"

"Who?"

"You know, the paleontologist who thinks he can bring extinct species back to life."

The idea makes me smile, but I have to keep my little sister's imagination in check. Otherwise she'll get herself kidnapped one day by the first man who comes along, scientist or not.

"What does Mike Archer look like?"

"I don't know," she admits, a little deflated. "Well, what if it's John Green or Quentin Tarantino—then can we?"

"Sash, we don't know them *personally*, we couldn't get into their car."

"You'd ruin my chance to meet a genius?"

"More likely I'd ruin your chance to be eaten by the Big Bad Wolf. Get it?"

She turns, mumbling something I can't hear. When a sleek black car appears on the horizon, her arms immediately shoot up and she waves them over her head.

The car comes to a stop just ahead of us.

"Oh, brilliant!" I mutter, annoyed. "Come over here and please stay calm, whatever happens."

I grab her hand as the door opens.

To my great relief, out steps my English teacher, Mr. Smith.

"Did I scare you, Phoenix?" he asks, playfully.

"No way!" Sasha pipes up. "Phoenix was lecturing me because she thought you were the Big Bad Wolf."

"No, I'm just Mr. Smith, her teacher."

I smile, embarrassed. I hate running into teachers

outside of school, especially the ones I really like. Without their handouts, they seem out of place, like bugs that scurry around, confused, when you lift up the rock protecting them from the sun.

"I love your T-shirt!" Sasha says, reading the quote written on the front. "'I believe in the night'—that's a verse from Rilke, right? One of my favorite poets. You have excellent taste."

"Th ... thanks," Mr. Smith stammers.

He looks at her, stunned, as if he might be hallucinating her. I think he's realizing what normally only I know: that she's the most extraordinary eight-year-old girl in the world. Everyone can see she's adorable, with that dreamy expression, that crooked smile, her curls, and her huge hazel eyes. But under that exterior is a brilliant mind and a unique personality that most people don't understand. Some call her "strange" because her intelligence makes them uncomfortable. Mr. Smith, though, seems delighted to have crossed her path.

"Come on, put your bikes in the trunk, I'll take you home. We can talk literature and cycling," he says, smiling.

The girls in my class are right: this man is way too charming to be a teacher. Hollywood doesn't know it, but tucked away here, in the middle of nowhere, is the reincarnation of a 1950s movie star.

"No thanks," I reply, blushing. "We live on the other side of the lake."

"So?"

So, we're about the only people who live over there, apart from fishermen and hermits. Few people risk driving there after sundown—too many deer to run over.

"I think Phoenix is scared to get in your Chevrolet because she finds you very intimid—"

I hastily cover Sasha's mouth. I feel my ears getting hot.

"Please, I'm sorry," I murmur. "We don't want to bother you, we don't live that far."

He smiles at me indulgently, as if I were an especially cute puppy. Before I can say a word, he grabs my bike and puts it in his empty trunk, on top of a plastic tarp. I hesitate to let go of my sister's bike. After all, I don't know Mr. Smith *personally*.

"I never eat little girls after six o'clock," he whispers to me, trying to keep a straight face.

I give in. It's strange to see him acting so casual, far from the scurrying bugs of his species.

The interior of the car is as impersonal as a hotel room: black and gray, clean and shiny. Even the keys hanging off the side of the steering wheel are held together with only a plain metal ring. Before starting the ignition, Mr. Smith turns to us in the back seat and politely but firmly tells us to be careful that our muddy shoes don't touch anything besides the rubber mat on the floor. We don't move a muscle.

"All right. Where to, ladies?" he asks, sounding like a limousine driver.

"The first mailbox you see, in twenty-five minutes," I say, hoping he can't see my face burn.

"Hmm, no wonder you're always late to my class."

"No, that's because Phoenix has a very individual sense of time," Sasha says. "She follows the cycles of the sun and moon, like the Maya."

Mr. Smith laughs. I've never heard him laugh outside our classroom. In the hallways, he always has the same expression as my sister when she's watching the news on TV—a sort of melancholy annoyance, as if life were nothing but a series of things that could go wrong.

I don't need to make conversation because Sasha has the gift of gab. She knows how uncomfortable I am speaking, how I prefer to stay quiet rather than risk embarrassing myself. Sasha, on the other hand, doesn't worry what people think, and she has a curiosity that comes out of genuine interest in other people, not just nosiness. So Mr. Smith replies enthusiastically to her interrogation. I learn that he doesn't know how to swim, draws blueprints for objects he never builds, loves Neruda's poetry but not Whitman's, and prefers Maggie to Bart Simpson and Snickers to Twix. That he had a difficult childhood in New England, and was planning to be a doctor until a family event prevented him.

Intrigued, Sasha presses for details. But now he seems to take offense at her interest, as if the small bit of information he's revealed has made him vulnerable. I see his shoulders stiffen and he changes the topic, expressing concern about our lack of interest in extra-curricular activities and clubs.

"Sometimes you have to force yourself to like things," he is saying, when, suddenly, we notice black smoke appearing above the trees. It's hard to tell, but it seems to be coming from near our house. Sasha stops talking and starts to look anxious. I'm not worried, though. I can't be, or let it seem like I am. I have to stay calm for the both of us. Sasha's stomach can detect tension better than a predator senses its prey, and her mood can change instantly at the first hint of something wrong.

As we get closer to home the clouds thicken. Sasha's breathing is speeding up and her jaw tenses. If Mr. Smith has noticed, he doesn't show it, and keeps on talking as if nothing's wrong. "So, tell me, how many wolves have you seen out here?" he says. When Sasha starts to gasp, I undo her seatbelt and pull her closer to me.

Our driver nervously glances back. At first I think he's concerned about Sash, but then I follow his eyes, which are focused on my sister's muddy boots on his clean leather seat. He faces front again and our eyes meet in the rearview mirror. He looks perturbed.

When we come to a stop sign, in a swift motion he brakes, turns around, and pulls off Sasha's red boots, one then the other, dropping them on the mat on the floor.

"That's better," he says, turning back and catching my gaze again in the rearview mirror. He smiles and steps on the gas.

I'm too stunned to say anything for a moment. Trying to get back to normal, I remember his question from a minute ago.

"We've only seen one wolf," I say. "A beautiful gray alpha."

"Oh yeah? Where was that?"

"The same spot where you found us."

"Now I know why you were so afraid," he says.

I'm not sure if he's talking about the alpha or himself. Maybe he's making fun of me; I can't tell. His expression is as mysterious as the Mona Lisa's.

"I wasn't afraid. Wolves only attack the weak."

"You don't think you're weaker than a wolf?"

"No, not when I've got Sasha and my father's gun."

Mr. Smith is on the verge of making a joke, laughter already lighting up his eyes, when we turn the corner and Sasha lets out a terrified scream.

TWO

I remember Sasha's first panic attack, three years ago.

I had found a drowned baby bird by the edge of the lake and I was excited to show it to my budding biologist sister, since it's very rare for a bird to die that way. All birds have the ability to float, thanks to their water-repellent feathers. But when Sasha saw its little body, swollen with water, she froze. Her eyes filled with tears. I started to feel guilty as she shook from head to toe, screaming.

After one long, final sob, she asked, "If I die, will it be forever too?"

"I have no idea," I said, truthfully. "No one knows what happens after you die."

I saw then the same fear I'm seeing in her eyes right now, unanswerable questions piling up like the smoke above our house. The bird's death had been the first shock, and from it sprang waves and waves of *why*s and *how*s. Since then, Sasha has become obsessively afraid of mysteries with no solution. Sometimes I have to remind myself that, even though her worries can be very adult, her irrational response is still like that of a little girl who's just been told fairies don't exist. I don't want to take away her innocence, just the violence of her reaction.

Thankfully, I've perfected some defense mechanisms against her panic attacks. I rub her temples and whisper formulas to soothe her. I talk about Newton's laws of motion, or Pythagoras's theorem. The precise, quantifiable logic of scientific theories always comforts her.

Sasha closes her eyes and I explain that combustion is a chemical reaction that requires three elements: heat, fuel, and oxygen—the fire triangle. When her breathing slows and her head settles on my lap, I realize the plumes of smoke aren't coming from our chimney but from behind the house, probably the garden.

"Do you think your parents are burning something?" Mr. Smith asks. He's speaking very softly, as Sash seems to be asleep.

"No, Erika's not back until Saturday."

"You have an older sister?"

"No, Erika's my mother."

He looks like he's waiting for an explanation, but it won't come. I'm a secretive person—"as secret as the recipe for Coca-Cola," Sasha always says.

When we reach the front of the house, Mr. Smith opens the back door of the car and takes Sash—still asleep—in his arms. If I tell people at school about this, I'll have more friends than Mark Zuckerberg on Facebook. Mr. Smith is a legend—students, parents, girls, boys, *everyone* agrees. You can't take your eyes off him in class, and he's the only teacher who writes comments on your report card that manage to sound both kind and enigmatic. The man has more facts than Wikipedia, and that's without mentioning his natural elegance, his perfect hair, or the dimple in his chin. But I decide I won't tell anyone at all, because "you don't get to 500 million friends without making a few enemies." I've observed my school environment enough to know that nothing makes enemies faster than jealousy, and also that a single enemy is enough to destroy your life. This is one of those things that's better to keep to yourself.

Mr. Smith insists on going in the house first, just to make sure the fire isn't coming from inside after all. I should tell him it isn't safe; flames would burn our dilapidated wood cabin to the ground as fast as if it were made of straw. But I don't stop him. I don't want to tell him that even turning on the lights in our place is a mortal risk.

Sasha is awake and standing now, holding my hand so tightly she's cutting off my circulation. As soon as we get inside, I notice that the fishing rods are gone from the display case in the entranceway. Sash notices too, and crushes my hand even more tightly. At the edge of the forest, a stone's throw from our garden's broken gate, Erika is crouching in front of the giant flames, too absorbed by them to notice our presence. You don't have to be Einstein to figure out that half the contents of our house are there in the center of the blaze. Mr. Smith lowers his head, obviously embarrassed to realize this fire was lit on purpose.

All of a sudden I realize it's Dad's things that are burning. Just his things.

It's all there: his fishing rods, the chair he liked to doze in after breakfast, the writing desk with the secret drawer where he kept the poems we wrote him for Father's Day. The African masks brought back from Ghana; the stacks of science magazines that used to flood the living room; the framed photos of him. His handmade stools. His drawings, which Sasha and I had hung on the walls of OUR room. His sweaters, his fishing vest ... and probably lots of other things, too, that we can't see because they're already reduced to ash.

"The boat," Sasha says, struggling to get the words out. "She took the rowboat."

I know I need to say something comforting, some words of strength, to stop her from crying. Consoling her is my specialty; it's what I do best. Except this time it's like I have a tree trunk in my throat, a dry trunk as big as a sequoia's.

"You can build another one, it's okay," Mr. Smith says, clenching his fists. "I could help you design it, if you want."

He smiles at us, careful to avoid meeting our eyes. Obviously not knowing what else to do or say, he awkwardly pats our heads and then leaves. I'm grateful to him for slipping out. This fire is too sad, too intimate for a stranger to see, no matter how well-meaning he is.

Needless to say we don't talk about the fire with Erika. She makes dinner in silence and we pick at it. Our appetites got lost somewhere in the ashes on the lawn.

There was nothing to save in the end, so there was nothing to say.

The truth is, since Dad left, Erika hardly talks to us. When she does, it's usually about bills or shopping lists or report cards. We've never been close, and I sometimes wonder if she wishes Dad had taken us with him—then she could make a clean break with the past, her children included. After all, she didn't have a choice where we were concerned. Dad left without saying goodbye, without leaving an address or a phone number. Like a master who abandons his dog at a rest area on the highway before going on vacation.

I have to admit Erika tries—though not hard enough—with my sister. Because Sasha, unlike me, isn't the spitting image of Dad. I'm the one who inherited his sandy blond hair that's impossible to style, and his pale, sad eyes. I have his voice, his shy, unkempt look, his way of walking "like a blue heron," as he always said—perching awkwardly on our long legs like swamp birds, but moving lightly, unnoticed, even in our big hunter's boots. I look so much like him that when I come near her my mother steps back, holds her breath, and crinkles her nose, as if I were the ghost of my father. *If I forget she exists, she'll eventually disappear*, she must tell herself.

I don't know who to blame anymore. We've never been able to count on our mom, it's true. But now Dad is somewhere else, out to sea, too far away to count at all.

THREE

Vanilla jumps on me in front of the school doors, quick as a gunshot.

"You lucky bum! So? Tell!"

It takes me three long seconds to realize she's referring to the Mr. Smith Incident and not the fire, which I haven't stopped thinking about. As Dad would have said, news travels faster than red ants in these parts. Especially if Vanilla is on the case.

"Sasha got a flat tire. He brought us home," I recap.

"And?"

"And he left."

"You're such a drag!" Vanilla exclaims. "What did you talk about?"

"He mostly talked to Sash."

"That doesn't surprise me! Did you sit next to him, at least?"

"No."

"If it had been me, I would have climbed into the passenger seat, right beside him," she sighs, "so close I could smell his aftershave, and then one thing would lead to another ... You think he's hot for you?"

"Do you really want me to answer such a stupid question?"

She laughs and gives me a gentle shove. The bell rings.

"You're not getting off that easily," she warns me.

I don't doubt it. Vanilla writes a blog, *Random Facts*, about our school, and she runs it like a CIA agent runs an interrogation. Few things escape her ears, and her hawk eyes have earned her the nickname "Big Brother"—as in "Big Brother is watching you." One time she discovered that our former principal was cheating on his wife with the former guidance counselor in the girls' restroom on the second floor. Quite the scoop.

Vanilla's good company, but I wouldn't go so far as to call her a "friend." For one thing, I don't have any friends apart from my sister, and for another, if I had to have one, I wouldn't pick Big Brother. I don't say that in a mean way. But everyone knows Vanilla's talents as an unscrupulous journalist prevent her from being loyal. She doesn't even understand the concept of friendship.

If I had to choose a friend, I'd pick her boyfriend, Dean, instead, who's smart and always recommends good books to her.

The first time Vanilla ever spoke to me, it was to ask my opinion of a book. "I'm in love with a bookworm," she explained, "and I heard you're the fastest reader in school." She needed me to give her summaries of the books Dean liked because she already belonged to four clubs, played three sports, and couldn't cut into her sleep time. Over the course of spending time together talking about novels, we ended up getting along. Even if I feel a little bad for duping Dean, I like being able to offer this kind of service. Dad always gave us lists and lists of things to read. "As long as there are books and plants, all will be well," he used to say, a doorstop of a novel in one hand and a garden hose in the other.

Every night, Sasha and I read books from Dean's lists of suggestions out loud together. Right now I'm reading Paolo Giordano's *The Solitude of Prime Numbers*, which has already earned a spot in our top three, between *Where the Wild Things Are* by Maurice Sendak and Chekhov's *The Seagull*. Before Sasha turns out the light, she insists on looking up the difficult words in the dictionary and then I explain any subtleties she's missed. In the morning, she loves to quote her favorite passages, often the same ones as mine.

Mr. Smith doesn't call on me once this morning, which is unusual given my spot in the front row. I prefer to be in the back, but he's got us seated according to his favorite plan: by rate of participation. The more often you speak up voluntarily, the farther away you're placed from the blackboard and the torture. With a rate of zero percent participation since the start of school, I've ended up farther into lunatic territory with each reshuffling. Now I'm between the class dunce on one side and the whipping boy on the other, directly in front of Mr. Smith.

Indifference is the worst punishment he can give. I'd much rather be the recipient of his famous Disappointed Look than endure his silent neglect. Still, I can't blame him for avoiding the daughter of a pyromaniac. If I were him, I'd do the same.

At the end of class, when I raise my head to look at him, he motions to me to approach. Feeling reassured, I quickly go to him. Vanilla makes an obscene gesture behind his back before leaving the room.

"Is everything okay?" he asks.

Part of me wants to tell him that ever since July that question has been on the blacklist of things you can say in my family. Because no, everything's not okay.

"Yes, great," I answer instead.

"I mean, *really* okay?"

I look at him, surprised. My sister is the only person I

know who cares about the well-being of people she barely knows, worrying about things like whether the cafeteria ladies are allowed to take the leftover food home at night. But Mr. Smith seems genuinely concerned, and that really touches me. That's why I don't answer; I don't want to lie to him.

The silence that follows is as uncomfortable as a scratchy tag on a sweater, but I hold my ground. He'll give in sooner or later; I'm unbeatable at this game.

Finally, he clears his throat. "Will your mother—I mean Erika—be at parent-teacher interviews on Monday?" he asks.

"Possibly."

"Can you speak in full sentences, please?" he reproaches me gently. "And can you get a definite *yes* by Monday? Because if I'm remembering right, she's never come."

Mr. Smith doesn't know that in my world mothers don't go to interviews, bake sales, or any other events that involve parent-child relations.

"Besides, I've written a superb report card singing your praises. Three pages, front and back, covered in hyperbole."

"Thank you, sir."

"No trouble, madam. So, is the bike fixed?"

"No, we took the bus."

I almost smile, remembering Sasha going up to the driver this morning and taking the seat behind him. She talked his ear off for the entire ride about an alternate route that could save passengers twelve minutes and forty-five seconds on a return trip. "Here's my scientific proof, for your boss," she finished, giving him a hand-decorated, sparkly pink envelope as we got off the bus. I'd bet my life that tomorrow the driver won't stop at our corner.

Now Mr. Smith seems lost in thought, staring at the paper-recycling bin as if he's trying to make it levitate or explode. I don't know if I've been given permission to leave so I wait, leaning with one shoulder against the blackboard.

"Stand up straight, please, you'll get yourself dirty," he finally says. "What time are your classes finished today?"

"Four-thirty."

"I assume you'll need to pick up your sister, so I'll come find you in the parking lot at quarter to five," he proposes.

I'm about to refuse when he raises his index finger.

"Sh-sh-sh, I didn't ask your opinion. And don't be late!"

FOUR

Vanilla is waiting for me in front of the restroom, her eyes hungry for secrets. Mr. Smith has been driving us to school and back all week, but I'm not talking to her now because it's Friday. And Friday is Baldini day.

I have to hurry because, at exactly ten o'clock, Marlon Baldini will cross the hall from the science lab to go to his swim training. I don't have physics or chemistry on Friday, and I definitely don't have swimming. Nevertheless, every week I make sure to "accidentally" find myself in this spot. I'm ashamed to admit it, but I know his schedule by heart. I stole it from a girl in his class. He's in A level, the sports track, the same as Dean. The same as all the popular guys.

Obviously I've never spoken to Baldini. We don't belong to the same cosmos. If one day a monarchy were established at school, he'd be the king, even above Mr. Smith. I, meanwhile, would be languishing in the slums, sharing my stale bread with the members of the magic club. Not that I want to be the queen, or even popular. I like being able to move around quietly without having to shake everyone's hand like a campaigning president. To be honest, I don't even understand the concept of keeping up an image. I'm always surprised by the scornful looks I attract with my lumberjack shirts and long, baggy pants with mud splattered on the legs. However, I don't really care, and everyone knows that. I might hang out with Vanilla, but I'm not one of those classmates you'll remember years after leaving school. And that doesn't bother me in the least. We children of the forest are just passing through.

So it makes no sense that *I* would like a guy like Baldini, the kind of guy who's the center of attention, doesn't take anything seriously, and always seems to be getting into a fight. On top of that, it's common knowledge that he goes through girls like they're chewing gum. I'm probably fooling myself to think he has more depth beyond his leather jacket, his perfectly messy blond hair, and his green eyes that can completely tear your heart out. Still, I feel connected to him.

I know I'm different from his many conquests and admirers for the very reason that I *don't* admire him.

Or at least, I don't think his attractiveness is the most important thing about him. I like the fact that even though we don't know each other, every week he gives me a sincere smile that says, "Hey, you're the Friday girl, I recognize you." Other girls would say I'm imagining things, and they might be right. The fact remains that he smiles at me—his white teeth flashing, his eyes lighting up without a trace of mockery. I have this sense that somewhere else, in a parallel dimension, or maybe even exactly right here, some deep feeling unites us. I don't know what it is, but it makes my head spin. Sometimes—I feel silly even saying it—our eyes meet as he enters the hall, and when we brush past each other, he looks twice as infatuated as me. Those days are electrifying. But make no mistake, I don't see the least sign that he intends to approach me—I'm not that arrogant. I'm just saying that he seems sweeter and more considerate than the rumors about him would lead you to believe.

Baldini is late. So late that it's difficult to look like I'm just passing here by chance.

I'm reading the fire emergency instructions for the fiftieth time when finally his head pops out from the crowd of students. I can't hide my amazement at how happy he seems just to be crossing the hall right now. He waves his hand excitedly to greet me, with the joy of someone who's spotted a loved one waiting for him

on a train platform. I can barely believe it. Before I do
something ridiculous like lifting my arm to wave back, I
glance behind me.

A pretty redhead who looks like Jessica Rabbit blows
him a kiss as she passes me, all smiles, stamping all over
my hope and dignity on her way.

I scurry away, counting the steps separating me from
my humiliation. It will take me a good million to recover
my pride—so many that my vision starts to blur.

How could I have waited six months before checking
to see if there was someone behind me? It must have
been *her* that Baldini was smiling at every Friday. There's
a good chance he never even noticed my presence, that
the feeling I was talking about was just my imagination.
In reality, I was nothing but Jessica Rabbit's shadow.

Sasha and Mr. Smith are standing by his car, chatting
like two old friends. She is telling him about her day,
in detail, every cafeteria item and sneeze included.
He's listening with intense concentration, as if she
were confiding state secrets. Even Dad doesn't have the
patience of my English teacher. You have to wonder if
he's putting on an act.

As we get in the car without a pause in Sasha's
monologue, for once in my life I'm grateful for my lack
of conversational skills. If I opened my mouth right

now, Sasha would guess immediately that something, or rather someone, has upset me. She'd question me relentlessly. In that way, she's like Vanilla, although my sister would end up finding just the right, funny words to comfort me. She'd say, for example, that boys are born with a smaller cerebellum than girls, which explains their lack of perception. She'd support this with an article written by an eminent researcher in *Science* magazine, and we'd discuss her work. Still, I'd rather she had fun with Mr. Smith. Sometimes she gets so absorbed in her books that she forgets she's only eight years old.

Sash has been seized with adoration for my teacher. Earlier this week, she told me that as of this month of April there exists in the world no one kinder or more devoted than he is. I can't argue with her. He comes to pick us up every morning and brings us home every evening, just so we don't have to wake up early and come home late. He feels it's his duty to see to our safety. I don't know why, but I'm glad to know there's one human being on this planet who cares we're alive. I almost have faith in adults again.

Vanilla, however, claims he's a dangerous serial killer and we won't realize it until it's too late. "No one is that nice to kids without an ulterior motive," she says. I can't help feeling that she hopes she's right, thinking of the material it would give her for her blog. She also says if she knew a murderer who was that attractive, she'd pray to all the gods to be his next victim. That's horrible, and typical of Vanilla's bad taste. Unfortunately, her twisted joke stays in my head and I can't help thinking about it when Mr. Smith turns to look at us, his forehead creased and his lips pursed.

"I'd like you to stop calling me Mr. Smith," he says to us. "Now that I've told you how much I cried at *Dumbo*, I think you should call me Jessup."

He did tell us that about *Dumbo*, it's true. But it's still hard for me to imagine him surrounded by piles of tissues, watching the mother elephant cradle her baby through the bars of her cage. I've never seen him get emotional about anything; according to all his students, that's his only fault. He's too cool to be sentimental.

"Jessup it is," Sasha says, and when we pull up to our house, they shake hands to seal the deal. I don't say anything, but when Mr. Smith—Jessup—holds out his hand to me, I shake on it, too.

A memory comes back to me, sharp as a drop of lemon on an open wound.

Dad would shake our hands whenever we made a silly bet. We'd make them constantly, betting we could do things the other two couldn't, each dare crazier than the last. For example, we had to read the last lines of a novel in the voice of someone famous, or hop on one leg in some unusual place, or guess the color of a polar bear's skin under its fur (strangely, black). I remember clearly that one week before he took off Dad told us: "I bet that neither of you loves me as much as I love you." We weren't sure how that could be a bet. How could we prove to our father that we loved him as much?

Well, now we've found out the answer. Sasha and I have proved our love for Dad every day since he's been gone. We wait for him, like termites that would rather die than desert their familial cocoon. And we take care of his plants, about the only things of his that Erika didn't destroy during her crazy pyromaniac episode. I'm sure she would have tried, but she couldn't get into the greenhouse, because I keep the key safe around my neck. If there's any place that symbolizes Dad to us, that's it. It's become our temple, our place of pilgrimage. Every morning, Sasha goes there. She checks which plants need water, repots the ones that are getting too big, and talks to all the sprouts, asking them to grow. After dinner, I do the same. There's no better proof of love than a healthy plant.

My dream is to find Dad sitting on the swing one evening, contemplating his orchids—in full bloom, thanks to the good care we've taken of them. Then we'll know he still loves us.

FIVE

We wait for the interview to end in the teachers' lounge,
which smells like stale coffee and photocopies. Sasha
managed to convince our mother to set foot in the school.
She said that Jessup was extremely keen on meeting her.
I think she's trying to play matchmaker.

It's not surprising the idea would cross her mind.
Erika was much more pleasant when Dad was around,
with the definite exception of the last few weeks
before he left, when they were fighting all the time and
talking about divorce. I'm not saying she was softer
or more affectionate before, but I felt like I knew her
a little better. She was different—happier, probably.
She participated in conversations, told doctor jokes,
awkwardly stuck bandages on Sash's skinned knees,
argued with Dad about how she got those skinned

knees, congratulated us on our growth after inspecting the latest measurements on the wall chart, read our horoscopes on Saturday mornings, and buttered our toast on Sundays. She never managed to remember our favorite kind of cereal or how many marshmallows we like in our hot chocolate, but she seemed to try. Now she's like a gust of wind that leaves behind nothing but a chill. She doesn't do anything for us. She doesn't do anything with us. She's content to pass through our lives and her own with total indifference.

None of this has surprised me, really. For almost seventeen years she's given me no good reason to call her *Mom*, and I've gotten used to it. I haven't expected anything from Erika for a long time. Sash is too young to abandon all hope, though. "If Mom is sad," she said a few days ago, "it's mainly Dad's fault." She's not wrong, in a way; we're not enough to make Erika happy. She's the type of person who needs a man in her life to be a better mother. And of all the men currently around, Jessup seems like the best choice.

"Jessup wouldn't be a good dad," Sasha announces suddenly, with importance.

I would love to be a neurologist so I could understand the complex workings of her brain.

"How do you know that?"

"Kids can sense these things, like animals," she explains, closing her eyes and breathing in deeply.

I'm skeptical. The last time she "sensed" something, we spent hours following the tracks of an imaginary caribou in the snow, got ourselves lost, and almost froze to death before finding our way back to civilization.

"Well then, it's lucky you already have a dad."

"*An absent father is not a dad.* We read that together, don't you remember?"

"Don't say things like that!" I exclaim, losing my temper. "Dad's been gone eight months, but for eight *years* he was the one who raised you. You don't have to read that in a book to know it's true."

Sasha looks at me for a moment, evaluating the intensity of my wrath. Then she takes my hand and kisses it—her way of admitting she was wrong.

I know she has the right to be angry with him—I'm angry with him too—but I can't stand hearing Dad talked about that way. Because he will come back one day. I'm certain of that.

"I just meant that Jessup would be more of a big brother," she says gently.

"You're right," I admit. "He's not the type to be a dad."

He's too young, too impulsive, too dashing. He doesn't have the patience to stay up all night tending a feverish child.

Sasha and I press our foreheads and noses together, making peace.

When the door finally opens, Erika has her hand on Jessup's shoulder, her head tossed back, a burst of laughter brightening her face. Her voice is pitched a little higher than usual, and my English teacher has never seemed happier. They look like a shampoo ad.

My sister does her victory dance, wiggling her pelvis and twirling her arms.

In the car home, Erika and Sasha rave about Jessup's many wonderful qualities. You'd think he'd cast a spell on them. I'm surprised to find their honeyed voices as irritating as nails on a blackboard. I like Jessup too, but everything's going too fast. Erika was supposed to *meet* him, not fall in love with him. I feel like I've witnessed Cupid's arrow at work. She's still grinning like a teenager. I don't remember ever seeing her this way with Dad.

"Jessup says if you use your full potential, you could get into a top university," she says to me proudly.

My "potential," meaning my free time. I've told him over and over that I have no intention of wasting that. I'd rather be pecked to death by magpies than fill out pages of registration forms for fancy universities with their pretentious admissions officers. If Dad were here, he would agree with me.

"Jessup says that you and Sasha are by far the most intelligent young people he's ever met," she goes on.

I focus on the grove of trees lit up by streetlights, trying to hide my annoyance. Erika has the irritating habit of brandishing us like trophies when she wants to make herself look good.

"Jessup could come over for dinner one night," she suggests. "What do you think?"

"I was just thinking that!" Sash exclaims. "He has to see our beetle collection."

I stay silent but note with surprise that Erika is being thoughtful enough to consult with us before acting. That's only happened once before: the day after Dad left. She was so lost that she asked us to decide whether we'd like to go to summer camp or stay home alone, since she'd be gone on business trips for much of the summer.

Which shows you how Mr. Jessup Smith has stolen her heart.

SIX

Jessup knocks on our door half an hour before the appointed time. Our mother curses because she's not ready. As the only member of the household not invested in a sacred mission in front of the bathroom mirror, I go downstairs to greet him.

"I was worried I'd be late," he apologizes, standing on the front steps and looking at his watch.

He's wearing the same black suit he wore for the parent-teacher interviews, possibly the only nice outfit he owns. I wonder if he's ever worn it to a funeral or a wedding. It's still a notable effort, since he usually wears a pair of black jeans and a faded T-shirt—and even that is the height of elegance compared to Dad's fishing getups.

"These are for the three of you," Jessup says, trying to loosen the knot of his tie.

He hands me some limp roses encased in an awful plastic film decorated with tacky red hearts. It's the kind of generic bouquet you find in bulk in supermarkets on Valentine's Day. But it's the end of April. Either he didn't go to the trouble of finding a real florist, or he doesn't know anything about plants. One way or the other, it's a bad sign.

I go to the kitchen and hurriedly shove the sad flowers in the garbage, then go down to the cellar to get a bottle of wine.

Jessup is sitting on the armrest of the sofa in the living room, nervously wiping his palms on his pants. I hand him the bottle, tied with a ribbon I found in Sasha's room. He freezes, clenching his fists.

"I ... I don't ..." he stutters, looking alarmed.

I'm not sure what to do. Mr. Smith is not in the habit of losing mastery of his words.

"It's just that Erika prefers wine," I explain to him, embarrassed. "Our dad grows flowers."

He exhales, like I've just told him he's been cured of terminal cancer. "Yes, of course," he says, taking off his sweaty jacket. "Thank you, Phoenix."

My eyes linger over his chestnut-colored business-man's shoes, polished to perfection. Our mother's shoes are always polished too. An idea crosses my mind. If people picked their partners just on the basis of similarity, Erika probably would have married Jessup without ever wasting time with our father.

"Do you want to see our room?" asks Sasha, wearing her uniquely hideous polka-dotted, frilly dress. She looks like a collector's doll, posed on a shelf between ceramic cats and porcelain shepherds. I shoot daggers at her with my eyes. Our room is a disaster and I have no desire to have my English teacher poking around in our private space. Too late. Jessup follows her up the stairs to the second floor. At the sight of the decrepit, stained walls, he swallows hard. Empty beige spaces have replaced the picture frames, leaving the rest of the wallpaper— once a shade called "English Cream"—looking dirty and yellowed. He scans our room without saying a word, though the wrinkle between his eyebrows creases a little more.

We haven't cleaned up like Erika asked us to. The piles of books at the ends of our beds form high, shaky walls, ready to collapse at the slightest misstep. On Sasha's bed, a notebook is lying haphazardly open, full of ideas, a gnawed pen stuck in the groove. On the imposing, somber wooden desk that's missing several drawers, my rough work for math problems, crumpled and torn, is strewn. An oak chair propped up with a piece of folded cardboard showcases our beetle collection and herbarium. Shoes, flippers, and roller skates are loitering solo in front of the window, their mates lost somewhere under the beds or in the closet.

"Please sit down," Sasha says politely, though I glower at her. Jessup slaloms through the junk over to my unmade bed, picking up my crumpled pajamas with his fingertips and moving them aside. I think about Vanilla, and how jealous she'd be if she were here. She'd probably beg me to never wash my sheets again.

All of a sudden, he's struck with a coughing fit; it sounds like he's going to hack up his trachea. My eyes fix on a bra hanging from the lamp on the bedside table, just a couple of feet away from my teacher's hand.

"I'm allergic to dust," he finally says.

Unfortunately for him, dust is the one thing our house isn't lacking. Erika never has time to clean, and we only do it when we figure there's nothing better to occupy our time, which wasn't the case today.

"The house is big enough that you could have separate rooms, isn't it?" he says, sighing at the dirty plaid shirts strewn over the brownish carpet.

"I don't wet my bed if Phoenix sleeps with me," Sasha states, with dignity.

One day, I need to teach her how to lie.

"She was having nightmares a lot," I say.

"Well, you have to toughen up," he reprimands curtly.

Sasha's face goes pale and she edges closer to me. He's frightened her. Immediately, he realizes it. Staring at the bunny pattern on my sister's bedspread, he smiles slightly, troubled, then quickly rubs his forehead, smoothing out his strained features as if he were wiping an Etch A Sketch clean. Only his gleaming eyes retain a trace of severity. He's the same way in class. He doesn't even need to raise his voice; Jessup is one of those teachers who just inspires respect. He has the charisma of a conqueror, almost like a figure from antiquity; like those legendary warriors for whom entire armies were willing to die.

His face now perfectly relaxed, he gets up and grabs a piece of paper.

"May I?"

I nod suspiciously, watching him fold, turn, and refold the paper until he's made an origami sailboat. He takes Sasha's hand and places the little boat on her palm.

"Can I still come over if it doesn't work out with your mom tonight?" he asks in a little-boy voice, a touch too smooth to sound sincere.

"Of course!" Sash exclaims. "Except if you're expecting to be paid like a babysitter."

He mimes an arrow going into his heart and collapses on my pillow.

"I'd do it even if I had to pay you," he says.

"Why?" Sasha asks, puzzled.

"Why?" He laughs loudly. "So your room won't look like this anymore!"

Erika calls us to dinner.

Watching Sasha and Jessup link arms, I have the feeling something new is taking shape. Unlike the rest of my family, I'm not at all ready to face it. I was fine with living indefinitely in the past.

For the first time in months, Sasha walks away without checking that I'm there by her side, and it claws at my heart.

SEVEN

Jessup and Sasha draw up plans for the boat. Every Wednesday after school, instead of marking papers, he shows her how to calculate, sketch, and improve their design. You'd think they were a couple of NASA engineers working on the next satellite to go into orbit.

I know I'm just being a killjoy, but I can't forget the old boat. The new boat won't be the same one we spent all our summers on, hiding behind the rushes and scaring tourists. It won't be the boat we sat in while Dad taught us to fish and count.

But when the design is ready, I swallow my grumbling and go with them to the sawmill.

A canvas-clad giant greets us at the entrance of a huge warehouse, which looks like an old converted barn. He's followed by a ball of fur that appears to be a cross between a lynx and a stuffed toy. The man is as frightening as he is large. Tall as a windmill, he has the damaged face of a war veteran. His left eye is almost hidden under what's left of a burnt eyelid. His right eye is barely open. A deep scar cuts brutally across his nose and forehead. I don't even want to imagine what his head looks like beneath his World Wide Fund for Nature ball cap.

Staring at him rudely, Sasha asks, "What breed is your dog?"

"There are no breeds of dog, just like there are no races of people," the colossus replies bluntly.

She blinks, speechless. It's quite a feat to render Sasha silent with no more than a few words, and I bow down before this heroic giant.

"To answer your question," he begins again, gently, "Pan is a Samoyed, a sled dog."

Sasha repeats *Samoyed* several times, stroking the furry beast.

As the ogre guides us between stacks of wood, I catch him glancing at me. Strangely, I feel completely at ease.

Jessup goes over to talk to a worker, leaving me alone with him.

"You're the little Cotton girl, aren't you?" the giant asks brightly.

I'm not sure of being "little," seeing that I'm almost seventeen, nine years older than Sasha, and five foot nine, but I nod. I am a Cotton: Phoenix Cotton.

"Ivan." He introduces himself, reaching out his hand.

That name vaguely rings a bell. He does look like one of Dad's typical friends—in other words, like a grizzly with dubious hygiene.

"Phoenix," I reply, squeezing his giant fingers.

"Strong like your dad," he observes, pleased. "How is he?"

I grit my teeth until my molars hurt. I don't like talking about him leaving. Telling other people makes it a million times more real. More painful.

Ivan sighs.

"Sailors who love flowers won't stay long away from their bowers," he predicts, placing his paw on my shoulder.

I've never met a poet who looks like a contract killer.

"It's been almost a year," I retort harshly, pulling away from his grasp. "And I've never seen you before."

"I wasn't in the area," he replies, defensive all of a sudden.

We look each other in the eye. His deformity can't obscure the kindness that exudes from him, his untamed-beast charm. He looks at me like his equal, like an adult.

"What happened to your face?" Sasha asks from behind us.

I grab her arm, signaling her lack of tact.

"It's a mask," Ivan jokes, "for next Halloween."

She approaches and tugs on his sleeve. He kneels down before her, bringing his face level with hers. Bewildered, he lets her examine him, caress each scar with her fingertips, tug at the damaged skin that is most definitely his.

Under her tender torture, he confesses. "I was hit by debris from a bomb I set myself, in a slaughterhouse."

"You're the eco-terrorist who went to jail!" Sasha exclaims, delighted.

Now I remember the newspaper clippings. Ivan Levy behind the bars of his cell. Dad told us often about the Earth Liberation Front, a group that sabotages companies exploiting the environment. He and Ivan were both members. He told us how on the night of the explosion the police arrested one woman and three men, yet only one of them—Ivan—was convicted, to serve as an example for the others. He did seven years in prison.

Dad had joined the group before he met Erika, for whom he abandoned his most extreme ideals. But he never told us if he was there that night in the slaughterhouse. It's one of those bitter family secrets, only brought up over dinners that end badly, when people have had too much to drink. I put together bits and pieces of the incident from reading some letters I found in Dad's desk, addressed to him. Maybe they were from Ivan. Maybe even sent from prison. They weren't signed.

"I was young and stupid," Ivan admits, his voice tinged with regret. "Your father already knew it then: family is the only thing that counts."

His ravaged face looks so sad that I feel the need to comfort him.

"Dad never used the word *eco-terrorist*. He preferred *angels of sabotage*."

Ivan looks away, but I think he's smiling.

"Does it hurt?" Sasha asks, gently.

"Only when I meet nasty people," he replies amiably.

"So is it hurting you now?" she says, mischievously.

"Absolutely not! And my scars never lie."

We smile.

Normally it takes me some time to adapt before I can be myself with someone I don't know. I'm not a naturally sociable creature like Sash. But there's something familiar about Ivan, and it makes me trust him blindly. He's simple, easy to read, like Dad. The exact opposite of Jessup, who's as cryptic as a quantum equation.

As if on cue, I hear the impatient honking of his car horn from behind the building. I don't want to leave. Not yet. Ivan comes up to me, pulls my hood over my head, and puts his hands on my shoulders. I don't blink, even though I normally hate strangers touching me. The gesture is pure and gentle. He searches for something in his many pants pockets, then hands me a business card for the sawmill with its slogan: *Gathered, not felled.*

"You can come here or call me any time, for any reason, okay?"

We nod, thanking him.

I hide the little card inside my jacket. If Jessup sees it he'll ask questions. He's even nosier than Vanilla. And he wouldn't understand. At the least mention of our father, he puts his hands over his ears to dissuade us from saying more. You'd think we were speaking of the devil.

In the parking lot, Jessup is talking with a tall blond boy who looks an awful lot like Marlon Baldini. Since it's too late to avoid him, I walk as slowly as possible. Sasha matches her pace to mine.

"Why are we moving like turtles? Do you know him?"

I stare at Baldini's dirty white T-shirt and pretend not to hear her. He looks so good, I feel like I've been teleported next to Brad Pitt in *A River Runs Through It.*

"He's handsomer than Jessup," Sasha says.

The inevitable is just a few feet away now. The sun glints off his blond hair and he looks like he's walked straight out of a documentary about California surfers.

"Hello," I mumble.

"Oh, hey, you're not gonna run away from me today?"

he says, surprised. "Is that because it's not Friday?"

He gives me that sly pout that makes all the girls at school go crazy. So I wasn't just a shadow. He did notice me every Friday.

Sasha crosses her arms and taps her foot impatiently, waiting for an introduction.

"Baldini goes to the same school as me," I explain.

"Marlon," he corrects, looking hurt.

"Cotton lives in the same house as me," Sash says, mocking me. "I'm the little sister, Sasha."

Marlon looks like he doesn't know if he should laugh; instead, he shakes her hand, smiling slightly. He looks at me, hesitating, then goes back to loading the last piece of wood onto the roof of the car.

Sasha takes my hand, murmuring, "Boys ... they're all cowards."

"Say thanks to your stepfather for me," Jessup says.

So Ivan is Marlon's stepfather.

"I will, sir. I hope Ivan and I can see your boat when it's finished," he says, looking at me. I become suddenly fascinated by the wood chips on the ground. I'm sure my cheeks have turned scarlet.

"If you swim in the lake this summer, you'll see it for sure," Jessup says, all smiles.

"I won't miss it," Marlon promises.

He opens the car door for Sasha, who gets in as slowly

and daintily as a Disney princess. Then he waves at me. I wave back, certain that this time there's no voluptuous redhead behind me.

"See you Friday!" he shouts over the crunch of tires on gravel.

In the car, Jessup and Sasha watch me, teasingly. I sigh loudly, contemplating the beautiful springtime scenery.

"Oh, don't worry, Phoenix, I fully approve!" Jessup exclaims. "His dental work is perfect, his IQ is more than respectable, and I'll even tell you a secret. The other day, I heard Annabelle Frost say that he kisses just as savagely as he fights. *Savagely!*" he imitates in a high, nasal voice.

Puckering her lips and raising her eyebrows, Sasha mimes a claw scratching the air.

We burst out laughing.

EIGHT

Erika has been home so much this month, we've been starting to wonder if she's been laid off. Usually she's on the road three and a half weeks per month, selling pharmaceuticals to doctors and hospitals. But since May, she's barely missed a weekend at home, buttering our toast on Sundays—to Sasha's delight—once again.

At first she pretended she was behind on some administrative files. Then she said it was a slow period at work. But I think the real reason is that she doesn't want to be away from Jessup. There's a symbiosis between them, like ants on an acacia tree. They finish each other's sentences so often you'd think they shared the same brain. Sometimes, when the window of our room is open, I hear her out on the deck, giggling. Before

Jessup, hearing Erika giggle would have been as unlikely as spotting a unicorn.

It must be said that my English teacher is a charming man, and not just because of his gifts as a pastry chef or his movie-star looks. Jessup couldn't be more perfect, and there's no doubt that our house is a thousand times nicer to live in when he's here. It's as if the floorboards suddenly stopped creaking and the hot water started flowing as soon as you turned on the tap.

Sasha even thinks he's ready for his immersion into the world of gore and zombies. I can't explain how my sister fell in love with horror movies, forcing anyone she deems worthy to sit through them with her. But she trusts Jessup enough to do him the honor of a proper initiation. This will consist of an atrociously bloody cinematic marathon, at the end of which he will be tested on his ability to drink a large glass of cherry juice.

"Listen up, Jessup," she declares pompously. "My dream is to play a cannibal zombie."

He looks up from the papers he's in the middle of marking. A touch exasperated by the intrusion, he says, "In that case, I'd recommend you watch *Night of the Living Dead.* When you turn sixteen."

Sash smiles at me as if this moment were the culmination of her eight years spent on Earth.

"I've seen it thirty-three times!" she cries, clapping her hands with joy.

"You're pretty young to watch that particular masterpiece, aren't you?" Jessup says, addressing me more than Sasha.

"I didn't force her to like zombies," I say, defensively.

He tends to think I'm setting a bad example for her, I've noticed. But my sister has never needed a role model for getting into trouble. At four, she was already making explosions, mixing together whatever incompatible ingredients she could find lying around. Jessup under-estimates her. Beneath that cherubic expression hides a swarm of diabolical ideas.

"I don't understand why kids have to wait to be adults before they can appreciate real art!" she states, indignantly.

She has a point, so he laughs, then considers.

"Have you finished your paper?" he asks me all of a sudden, looking at his watch.

"The one on Lincoln? No, we agreed I'd do it by the end of the week."

He studies me coolly, as if he's thinking *I hope you're not lying to me.*

"But I have finished the two essays and the multiple choice questions on the Civil War," I add.

"Good, except you were supposed to do Lincoln first."

Ever since he started spending most of his weekends here, Jessup's taken a grim pleasure in interfering with our academic lives. Especially mine, since Sash is only in grade three and already knows more than most of her teachers. Far from being the cool Mr. Smith I used to know, Jessup now assails me with "bonus work," as he calls the piles of quizzes and essays on every subject that he designs "just for you and your future." Besides that, he's made me a martyr in English class, interrogating me constantly and taking marks off my average if I make the slightest careless mistake. According to him, it's unacceptable for my grades to fall short of my intellectual capacities. "It's a waste. I never had a choice; I didn't grow up in a loving, cultured family," he told me acidly. "But from what you and Sasha tell me, your father was an extraordinary man." Yes, I want to say—and he still is. He is because he never pushed us to perfection. He always thought it was more important to learn to recognize different types of insects than to be able to blindly recite the birth dates of presidents. And I agree. As long as my homework is done and my grades are okay, I feel I have the right to choose my own things to learn, not limit myself to some instructions on a page. I'm not asking for permission to be lazy. I just want the freedom to explore life beyond the same old lessons they've been harping on for decades in school.

"Okay, we'll look at your homework when we get back," Jessup says, yielding, before he disappears down the hall.

I stick out my tongue at Sasha. *Phew!* she mouths, one hand wiping her forehead. It's not easy to escape our new private tutor.

Half a second later he reappears, holding our coats in one hand and our shoes in the other.

"We're going on an adventure. I have something amazing to show you!" he says.

Jessup loves going off on long, surprise car trips. He gets a thrill out of finding a new restaurant on a country road, buying Erika a present in some offbeat place, or visiting strange museums.

With a mysterious look, he puts on his raincoat, winking at us. We take the road heading to the next town, ending up near an abandoned shopping mall. Behind a building under construction, we discover a huge shop filled with zombie masks, vampire costumes, and other horror-themed accessories. I think Sasha is about to pass out from excitement. The saleswoman's *Exorcist* makeup is so convincing that I wouldn't be shocked if she vomited on us while spinning her head around 360 degrees.

Jessup and Sasha spend nearly an hour wandering the aisles among the faces with gouged-out eyes and the hanging guts, trying on masks and bizarre outfits, laughing at themselves in front of the distorting mirrors. Finally they decide to buy two enormous bottles of viscous, lumpy red liquid, a plastic saw, some candies shaped like vital organs, and some bits of human body parts that drip blood when you squeeze them. The saleswoman graciously gives us a bunch of black wigs and a jar of white makeup for free before wishing us a macabre rest of the day.

Braving the rain, we dart over to a secondhand store, looking for cheap clothes to test the fake blood on. Instead, we leave with a scarf for Erika and a copy of *Back to the Wild: A Practical Manual for Uncivilized Times* for me and Sasha. Jessup never buys anything for himself. "It's how I was raised," he explained once, looking serious.

When we get home, he and Sasha put the finishing touches on their zombie costumes, dribbling toothpaste mixed with corn syrup down their chins. I take the opportunity to go out to the greenhouse and turn up the temperature. But as soon as I close the door, two horrors appear from out of nowhere, eyes rolling back in their heads and severed fingers dangling from their mouths. I giggle hysterically as they chase me through the garden, slipping on the carpet of mud.

Quick as a shot, I go back in the house, throwing myself on the couch with relief. My fingers reach for the remote, but suddenly Jessup is there, standing in front of the TV.

"No, no, no, Phoenix. Not until you've finished your essays and cleaned up the mud on the floor."

"It's only five o'clock, we'll clean later," says Sasha, out of breath.

Jessup places his fists on his hips and I stare at the ceiling as he launches into his umpteenth speech about the importance of punctuality, of doing a job well, et cetera, his voice cooler than a block of marble. He's a total stickler for schedules, putting the White Rabbit in *Alice in Wonderland* to shame. Sasha was the one who first noticed the resemblance, and since then it's been our little joke.

We look at each other and sing:

I'm late! I'm late! For a very important date!

The tension leaves Jessup immediately. He shakes his head, his frown becoming a smile. Playing along, he imitates the panicked rabbit, pointing at the living room clock and pretending to serve us tea.

He goes to the kitchen to get three pieces of the Black Forest cake he made the night before to "broaden our culinary culture," then joins us on the couch.

"Listen, we'll watch *Attack of the 50 Foot Woman* and after that you'll attack your homework, okay?"

"Okay," we reply, mouths full.

Sasha and I weren't wrong about Jessup: he's the big brother we always wanted to find under the tree on Christmas morning. Although in my childish imaginings he was a little less strict, and a lot less attractive.

NINE

We finish mowing Mr. Werts's lawn, our tenth one this week. Lawn mowing marks the beginning of summer, the arrival of tourists, and a way to earn some pocket money. We've made enough this week to go on a spending spree at Bertha's Videos—the only DVD rental store in the whole area that hasn't shut down, and a peaceful, quiet place where Sasha has no choice but to shut her mouth. I especially like to take her there on days when she's giving me a headache.

Bertha, the owner, considers her store a sacred place. "You'll find more gods here than in church," she tells anyone within earshot. We usually go once a month—with a strict budget, since Sash doesn't know how to restrain herself. And we make sure to pick a day when Erika isn't around, because she hates Bertie—a childhood friend of Dad's, and the one woman there the night of the explosion with Ivan.

We, however, adore her. She's vivacious and delightfully rude and knows more about movies than anyone. When she's in a good mood, she lets us watch films from her private collection. We sit together on the ground, on an old, soft, reddish carpet that smells like popcorn. I like doing my homework there, below the shelves of foreign classics, with all the great directors watching me solve my equations.

Sasha stops me in my tracks. Jabbing my hip with her elbow, she whispers, "It's the golden boy."

I nod and swallow audibly. My saliva feels like molten lava.

We hide between the Action Films section and the Musicals shelf, eavesdropping on the conversation.

"I'm still waiting for that snowboarding documentary I asked for last month," Marlon is saying.

"And I'm still waiting for you to act like a man. Apparently neither of us is going to get what we want today," Bertha replies, scathingly.

Sasha giggles and pushes me toward the candy display stand, three feet from Marlon. He turns and gives us a big, gleaming smile. Slouched in a chair behind the checkout, Bertie wiggles her plump fingers hello.

"You're just in time, my little chicks. You can be my witnesses. Listen!" she exclaims, pointing a menacing index finger at Marlon's nose. "Your mother told me what you've been up to. You don't think she's gone through enough? You should be ashamed of yourself! You'd better change your attitude now or I'll have something to say!"

He looks back at us over his shoulder, his face crushed, as if we've just seen him with his pants down getting spanked. Bertha must be referring to his latest scrap. He's still got a bit of a shiner and a bandage over his eyebrow.

Sasha goes up, puts her elbows on the counter and her chin in her hands. She looks straight at Marlon.

"You have to show them you're sensitive," she advises. "Women detest brutes."

"I'm not a brute! I swear, I'm done with all that," he says, looking at my sister tenderly. "See, I'm good now."

"Oh, really? Which fairy waved her wand over you?" Bertha grumbles.

He stands up straight and nods toward me. Me? What have I done to get involved in this? If that was a joke, it's a cruel one, worthy of Vanilla. I didn't think Marlon was like that.

Bertha clears her throat. "You're not good enough for her, honey," she says.

"Not yet, I know. But I will be," he says, seriously.

"And the chosen one, what does she think about this?" Bertie asks me.

The chosen one?

Marlon turns to me, raising his eyebrows. *Don't look at him, think about something else*, I tell myself. Suddenly Bertha sneezes. Perfect. *The world record for the fastest sneeze is 103 miles an hour, twice as fast as a dragonfly at top speed.*

"Phoenix thinks Marlon is like the Great Gatsby," Sasha blurts, tossing a gumball into her mouth.

He looks at me skeptically. Bertie bursts out laughing, her chest trembling like jelly.

"That's nothing to laugh about!" Sash adds. "She'd make a great Daisy Buchanan, if she weren't so smart."

I swear to myself to never, ever tell her a secret again. I pray that Marlon's never read the book or seen one of the five movie adaptations, because if he has, he must be laughing at me. Romeo's love for Juliet pales next to Jay Gatsby's love for Daisy.

It's better if I don't take my eyes off the carpet. As mortified as Kafka's cockroach, I scurry away behind the curtain of the Asian Cinema section. I take out my physics textbook and start reading about atomic collision, burying myself like a mouse inside its hole.

I don't emerge again until I hear a car pulling into the parking lot, and the familiar sound of Jessup's horn. Bertie rises up out of her chair and crosses her arms. Marlon is still at the front, frowning as he flips through an issue of *American Cinematographer*.

"Who's that?" Bertie mutters, on guard.

Marlon looks up from his magazine. "Him? That's Mr. Smith, the English teacher. He's cool," he says. "He's your stepdad, right?"

I nod. Although technically I prefer the term "provisional big brother."

"He looks like the Norwegian," Bertha observes, flatly.

Marlon freezes, his eyes like two black holes. It seems Sasha and I are the only ones here who don't know who "the Norwegian" is. We don't ask, as from the looks on their faces, it's not a nice person or a pleasant memory.

As Jessup enters and greets them politely, I sense an arctic chill spread through the room. I pick up the bag containing our ten DVDs and pull the Norwegian's doppelgänger toward the exit before he gets himself killed.

They don't say goodbye.

"Jeez, that woman could kill you with a look," Jessup

says once we're outside. "Your mother's right, you shouldn't be alone with that nut. It's like a real-life horror movie in there. I don't trust her."

I don't understand why, but the feeling is obviously mutual.

TEN

We got two big pieces of news this week. I wish I could say the second was as happy as the first.

On Monday, when we woke up, the newly built rowboat was shining on the dock. It was tied with a huge red ribbon, the kind you might see on a BMW for a rich kid on graduation day. It was a surprise, because Jessup had told us the boat wouldn't be ready for this summer. What with end-of-year exams, advising students, and preparing for next year, he'd said, he wouldn't have enough time to help us. "Summer holidays without a boat are like ... Watson without Holmes," Sasha had complained, her face as sad as a rainy day. I'd felt the same; we might as well skip from spring straight to fall.

Jessup must have been working alone, probably when we were out fishing, maybe even at night.

The little boat is painted royal blue, just like the old one, and inscribed on it in red are the words: "This is not a boat." Which makes us laugh like hyenas. A few weeks ago Sasha discovered the famous painting by Magritte of a pipe, with the words "This is not a pipe" written below it. It's been a game between the three of us ever since. *This is not a teacher. This is not a movie. This is not my sister. This is not a lake.*

So our boat is a masterpiece—Jessup has outdone himself. He's earned a million points on the Provisional Big Brother scoreboard. And not just because of the boat, but because of the time and care he spent on it. Another few million points and we might adopt him.

The second piece of news was so unlikely it could have made us believe in the existence of Santa Claus and the resurrection of the dinosaurs, the Tasmanian tiger, and every other extinct species all at once. It was one of those things that's so unexpected it almost makes you cry.

The postman rang the doorbell this morning, the first of July, one year since Dad left. My birthday. In spite of the pretty blue boat, the beginning of summer vacation, and the cake with seventeen candles, the atmosphere wasn't particularly festive. He handed me a square, apple-green envelope, the kind you'd use for an invitation to a kid's birthday party, and was already gone by the time I

opened it to find a postcard from the Falkland Islands—
our first card from Dad! Up to that point, we only knew he
was still alive because of the money he put into Erika's
account every month.

On the back of the postcard was written: "Follow the
bluebird all over the world, but you'll only find happiness
where you started from." One of Sasha's favorite quotes.
Seeing Dad's chicken-scratch handwriting again, I felt
overwhelmed. Beneath the quote, he had sketched a man
on an island, crying, and it was signed, "Salty kisses,
Dad." I flipped the card from back to front. No apologies.
No "Happy birthday, Phoenix." No explanation, and
definitely no address. It was like someone gently kissing
your forehead while they stabbed you in the back. Now
that we knew where he was, now that we'd heard from
him, I realized that this wasn't actually what I was
waiting for. What I wanted was for him to miss us so
much that he'd phone, that he'd come back. We'd dreamed
of his return for so long, and then ended up with one
sentence that he didn't even come up with himself,
hastily scribbled on a piece of cardboard.

"Maybe he has that strange disease that makes you
forget things every two minutes," Sasha diagnoses.

"I doubt Dad has turned into a pigeon."

"The disease exists," she says. "I read about it in *The*

Strange World of Medicine when we were at the library on Thursday. Remember, when you were doodling on the table because you were fed up with Jessup's corrections? And the lady told you to stop or she'd have to tattoo your forehead. And you told her that she could—"

"I remember, Sash," I say, cutting her off. "And I believe you. But I don't think Dad's problem is amnesia."

She thinks for a minute. "If there's no rational explanation," she says ominously, "then it's even worse."

"I know," I say. "At least he's writing us now."

But disappointment tunnels through my stomach.

"You still have presents to open, remember?" Sash suddenly asks, feigning enthusiasm.

I smile, less cheerfully than I should. I've been holding back tears for fifteen minutes, and my face crumples. Sasha won't let go of my hand, which is damper than a tropical forest. A few tears escape our eyes. We wipe them away quickly with the backs of our hands—and that's it. All that Dad deserves. From now on we won't expect anything more than postcards.

Sasha stays silent until she can't hold her words back any longer.

"This is not a father."

I smile, then wrap my arms around her, as soft as a marshmallow.

"You are the best birthday present anyone could ever have, and I think that every year," I breathe into her hair, which smells like humid earth.

"What about a Christmas present?" she asks, faking offense. "I'm not your best Christmas present? And Valentine's present? And Thanksgiving? And Hanukkah?"

We laugh, a laugh that soothes after sharp pain.

Trying to take our minds off the painful postcard, Jessup calls us into the living room. Erika pulls the curtains shut. She'd been saying she really wanted to be home for my birthday, and here she is. Somewhere, under the hurt of all the other important days she's missed, that cheers me up. She's made an effort. For me.

The television is the only light in the room and it stipples our faces.

"We're going to have a horror movie marathon and eat popcorn until it comes out our noses!" Jessup states gleefully.

Exactly what we need: blood and salt.

"I'll go find *Night of the Living Dead*!" Sasha shouts, already in the hallway.

"We have a present for you," whispers Erika, not used to saying that sort of thing.

Sasha returns, pushing a strange kind of trolley. It

has a little window with what looks like a sign, but it's too dark to see. It looks like a hot dog stand. Erika turns on the lights.

"This way you won't have to visit Bertha!" she proclaims.

A popcorn machine! A vintage model, the kind you only see now at fairs and in old neighborhood movie theaters.

"Thank you," I whisper. I mentioned this to Sash months ago. Back in January, I read in *Treasures of Hollywood Cinema* that real cinephiles always have a collector's item, whether it's an old film reel or a popcorn machine. The two of us searched the internet for hours. The prices were ridiculous. We would have had to mow every lawn in the region.

"I bribed three contortionists and a bearded lady to get this little gem," Jessup announces proudly.

"I can vouch for that, I was there," Erika adds with a complicit smile.

She looks so happy that I hug all three of them. It hasn't felt this warm here for such a long time. Sasha hugs us back even harder.

"If an old piece of junk makes you this happy, we should do a tour of the flea markets!" Jessup exclaims.

I look at Erika. I think she may be too stunned to talk. We haven't hugged her since last fall.

She'd come home one night in October to find the living room clean. No more trace of the tissues she'd used to dry her rivers of tears. Her room was tidy, her bed made. We had changed the sheets and gotten rid of the half-empty cups of coffee cluttering her table. There was no more expired food in the fridge. I'd had enough of Vanilla's comments when she came over: "Are you sure your mom won't hang herself with all those tissues?" Or, "Nothing more fun than a study session in a haunted house!" So Sasha and I had put the house in order, made it look like we were no longer in mourning. But Erika shouted that we were selfish, that we had no right, especially not in *their* room. Sash protested and cried, but Erika walked out of the house, slamming the door. Two hours later, she came back, offering a candy apple in each hand, and we embraced.

Remembering this, I understand the fire in April a little more. It wasn't the smartest idea and she should have at least warned us first. But she thought she was doing the right thing, trying to erase her pain and ours, or at least the visible traces. Trying to free us from that awful first of July, one year ago today.

ELEVEN

Jessup watches anxiously as we untie the rope from the boat to the dock.

"Come back for snack time," he shouts. "There'll be waffles!"

From the kitchen window, he waves his hand like he's just been crowned Miss Universe.

We wave back, then push off.

Jessup avoids the lake as much as he can. He has an impressive fear of water. A TV report on anything ocean-related can give him cold sweats. He confessed to us once that he hated our bathroom. "That old bathtub is as terrifying as Hannibal Lecter," he whispered with his back to the tap, like he was afraid of being overheard. Ever since, Sasha always says she's going to run herself a "Hannibal full of bubbles."

The other side of the lake is where the tourists stay, in the hotels and bungalows and villas for rent. We see them sometimes, awkward in their paddleboats and canoes. We never go over to their side, which has been designed for their comfort with artificial sand and blue-and-white-striped beach towels.

Thankfully, the lake is pretty big and the undesirables don't venture into the places hidden behind the reeds.

We always tie up our boat within a few miles of home, on the edge of a field of wild cotton grass, with its fluffy candy-floss heads that tickle Sasha's legs. "A perfect spot to watch *Calopterygidae* dragonflies and *Homo sapiens* nudists," Dad used to say, a pair of binoculars around his neck. It's always been our little piece of paradise. We tied a rope around the highest branch of a beech tree next to the lake so we could swing from it, like Tom Sawyer and Huckleberry Finn bounding into the Mississippi.

But today, as we pull up to our refuge, we hear a dog barking and voices reciting lines from a familiar play.

"It's *The Cherry Orchard*, by Chekhov," Sasha says.

My sister's love of theater is second only to her love of zombies.

We hear a woman's beautiful voice ringing out passionately: "*Cut down the cherry orchard? My dear, excuse me, but you don't understand at all! If there's one*

71

thing interesting or remarkable in this whole province, it's our cherry orchard."

Before anyone can respond, Sasha continues: "*The only remarkable thing about your orchard is that it's big. It only bears cherries every other year, and even then you don't know what to do with them; nobody wants to buy them—*"

"Shh!" I interrupt, putting my hand over her mouth.

I try to push the boat away, but it's too late.

"Who's there?" the woman's voice asks.

Anyone who can recite Chekhov is a friend of Sasha's, so she grabs the paddles, guiding us between the bulrushes and reeds. A woman as delicate as tissue paper catches the edge of our boat. To her left is Ivan, holding a warped, dog-eared copy of *The Cherry Orchard* in one hand. Not far away, Marlon stands, a fishing rod resting by his bare feet.

"So that's why I haven't been able to catch a single fish," he says.

"Don't blame us," Sasha replies, laughing. "Fishing is all about technique. Either you've got it or you don't."

That's what Dad used to say.

Ivan and the delicate woman laugh. Marlon joins in, and comes over to help us tie our rope to the ring in the ground. It looks like he hasn't had much practice with boats or sailor's knots. I take the rope from his hands, ignoring his look of defeat, and tie the knot expertly.

"Years of experience," Sash says.

He nods. His arms hang loosely by his sides and his cheeks are rosy.

"Phoenix, Sasha, this is my wife, Prudence," Ivan says, lifting my sister out of the boat.

That name—*Prudence*—sounds like all the elegance in the world. I doubt any other woman could wear it so well.

"I've heard a lot about you," she says, hugging us affectionately.

Her eyes are as green as Marlon's, but that's where the resemblance ends. She's so slight she looks like a teenager in her big overalls. For a flash, I get the sense I'm seeing the adult version of Sasha: she has the same chestnut curls, same little ears that stick out, same bitten fingernails, and most of all that same look of being somewhere else. You'd almost expect to see a fairy alight on her frail shoulders.

"My favorite play is *The Seagull*," my sister says, stroking the dog, which wags its tail.

"Mine too!" Prudence exclaims. "In fact, I'm planning to put it on next year with the drama club."

Those words, *drama club*, are the key to Sash's heart. She looks at me imploringly, a smile spreading across three quarters of her little face.

"It's Sasha's dream to work on a play," I say shyly.

"You can help with ours, I hope!" Prudence says enthusiastically. "There'll be sets to decorate, props to make ..."

Sasha nods excitedly, and can't resist the urge to fling her arms around Prudence. The instant affection seems to go both ways, so I don't hold her back.

While they discuss costumes and lighting techniques, I study Marlon's fishing rod with scientific intensity.

"He doesn't have the right reel," I whisper to Ivan, who's collapsed in a lawn chair. "With that type of line, he needs a fly-fishing reel."

"Exactly what I told the guy," he says loudly.

Marlon sits down beside me, all ears. My nostrils fill with a honey-sweet scent. A cheap girl's perfume. Usually when I pass him in the hall, he smells like tobacco and chlorine.

"So, Friday. Why don't you ever talk to me?" he asks, in his most charming tone.

I watch Ivan pick up his chair and move under the shade of the beech tree, leaving us alone. I'm trapped.

"We don't ... we don't know each other," I mumble nervously.

"Of course we know each other, Miss Daisy Buchanan! *He was consumed with wonder at her presence.*"

So he's read *The Great Gatsby*. He beams at me like a

kid bringing home a test with a perfect score.

If I could politely escape from this conversation, I wouldn't hesitate for a nanosecond. It's one thing to imagine talking to someone in your wildest dreams. It's another to make a fool of yourself in the flesh.

"I borrowed the book from Dean after hearing Sasha talk about it," he says. "You've read it, I guess. Obviously, you've read everything."

"Not everything," I demur.

His fingers graze a bruise on my knee, then slide down my calf. The hairs on his arm are standing on end. The sun's heat is blistering and I might be imagining it, but the crickets seem suddenly overexcited.

"I've noticed you, you know ... at school," he whispers, inches from my neck. He's so close I can detect the scent of his cinnamon chewing gum. I think about Vanilla, who says the best way to shut a guy up is to stick your tongue in his mouth. I don't reply, so he goes on:

"I know you have a little scar shaped like a branch on your left arm. Here," he says, touching it gently. "You borrow the same books as Dean from the library, and I'm pretty sure you're the one who explains them to Vanilla. She couldn't come up with anything that good on her own. But don't worry, your secret is safe. What else? Your locker is the tenth—no, the eighth—from room 345, next to Annabelle's. And you always have this mysterious key around your neck."

I swallow the tiny bit of saliva I have left as he gazes at me.

All charmers have their tricks. Marlon is observant, nothing more. I try to focus on the nauseating scent wafting off him, which probably belongs to Annabelle, his last trophy. Or maybe that Jessica Rabbit girl. I'm not the type to believe in miracles, like the miracle that he's suddenly fallen in love with me. At the most, maybe he's looking for a fling over the summer because it's hot, he's bored to death, and his real prey are all off on vacation. When September comes, he'll pretend not to recognize me, I'll go back to being a shadow in the hall, and it will break my heart all over again. I've watched him, too. I know how Don Juan operates, how sincere and alluring he can seem. It's better if we're just friends.

"*There is no remedy for love but to love more*," Sasha announces solemnly.

Marlon jumps up, turns red, then sits back down next to his fishing rod.

I'm going to drown her.

"How many times have I told you not to eavesdrop on other people's conversations?" I reprimand her.

Sash sticks out her tongue. She's even touchier than Jessup.

"You don't need to go around quoting Thoreau," I add.

"You're smart enough to come up with your own words."

Marlon is vigorously pulling clumps of grass out of the earth, looking hurt. He must think I'm criticizing him, too, for his Gatsby quote.

"Don't you think it smells like air freshener around here?" my sister asks with a little cough.

Marlon laughs and sniffs his stained T-shirt.

"Yeah, it's me," he admits, grimacing. "I was trying to buy some perfume for my mom's birthday."

And not for Annabelle Frost's, I think, relieved.

"Phoenix just had her birthday on July first!" Sasha informs him.

"Oh, I didn't know," he says, looking apologetic.

"It doesn't seem like you know much about her," Sash notes disdainfully. Her contemptuous air reminds me of Jessup when he's making fun of the other teachers at school. I look at her sharply and she understands immediately that she had better be nice. I'm not joking around.

"You're totally right. I need to catch up," Marlon says.

No, I shake my head, there's nothing to catch up on. If he keeps being so nice I'm going to start getting ideas.

"No perfume," Sasha advises. "Phoenix likes personal gifts like drawings, made-up puzzles, rare films, or hand-made things. Except last year, it was different because our dad left, so she—"

I glare, stopping her cold. Drowning won't do it this time; I'll have to cut her up into tiny pieces and eat her. There's a screenplay idea she'd love.

"I get it. Something unique," Marlon says, pondering.

"No, you really shouldn't bother," I insist.

He smiles at me, his Friday smile.

After a quick jump in the lake, Ivan and I have a long talk about Dad. It's so nice to hear new things about him, like discovering a trunk full of family photos in the attic that you didn't know existed. But, at 3:30, I remember Jessup, and we have to take our leave. Obviously Jessup's waffles are just a pretext to make sure we come back safe and sound and on time, or else risk spending the rest of the day buried in our workbooks.

Sadly, we won't see the Baldinis again until the end of August. They're going camping in the mountains. Sasha looks as if she wishes they could take us along in their backpacks. And as far as I'm concerned, if they wanted to pop up like wildflowers again in our private spot on the lake, it wouldn't bother me—just the opposite.

As we push off from shore and start paddling back home, I look at Ivan, Prudence, and Marlon receding into the distance, and wonder if maybe we've found our second family.

TWELVE

Jessup told us he had to go back East for a while. He was
vague when Sasha asked him why he had to leave so
quickly. He said something about sorting out a family
issue, muttering curses about his father. Erika didn't
seem fazed. He's a reserved, mysterious man, and she's
not the type to make a scene in public—meaning in front
of her kids—or even in private, I think.

He's called us five times in the last week. I'm touched
by the attention, especially since he isn't a big talker. He
said he wanted to hear "friendly voices" and told us about
the butterflies in the botanical garden he visited. He also
wanted to check that we were making the most of "the
glorious month of July"—without neglecting our summer
reading lists.

Which is exactly what we've been doing—enjoying the summer, that is.

In the mornings, we race around on roller skates, on skateboards, or hopping on one leg. Sasha even managed a staircase descent without a bruise. When night falls, we launch fireworks from the garden: red dragons, Bengal tigers, and other ferocious beasts roaring among the stars. Bertha gives them to us for free. "Anything to scare away the tourists," she says. Bertie's just sick of people coming in and demanding superhero movies and rom-coms. We often visit her after breakfast to give her a distraction, asking for recommendations of films by her favorite directors. Once in a while, feigning innocence, she asks questions about Jessup, but refuses to answer Sasha's about "the Norwegian." She says Marlon will talk about it one day. "If he wants to become a man, he won't have a choice. And when he's ready, you'll be the one he'll tell," she assures me. *To become a man*—it sounds like a line from a movie. And I don't understand why Marlon would want to confide in me.

Sasha and I buy new plants for Dad's greenhouse. At first mostly carnivorous ones, to battle an invasion of flies. But the voracious plants grow abnormally fast and start threatening the orchids, so we get rid of them quickly. Even afterward, though, there is no longer a fly in sight, either inside the greenhouse or out. Sasha says word must have gotten out; we should grow an army of carnivorous plants to keep away big predators like foxes and bears. "Or dangerous men like Mr. Smith," Vanilla adds jokingly.

She comes over to hang out with us some evenings, when she needs the boat for her nocturnal escapades with Dean. In exchange, she brings us gigantic tubs of ice cream with tempting names like Crazy Caramel Fudge Lovers or Marshmallow Triple Chocolate Explosion. Sometimes she sleeps over at our house, which makes her an ideal victim for Sash. My sister waits in the bedroom with the lights off, made up like an extra from *Zombieland*, then jumps out from behind the door with her arms stretched out in front of her, moving jerkily. Last night, she gave Vanilla such a shock that she was shaking like someone having a seizure. We all laughed until our stomachs cramped.

In the month since my birthday, twelve postcards from Dad have arrived. Each one came sealed in an apple-green envelope, as if to protect it on the long journey, and on the inside, each had a quotation and a drawing. They came, in order, from the Strait of Magellan, Puerto San Julián, and Puerto Lobos—four cards from each spot. Each card is different, and I like to imagine our father scouring the coastline for miles in search of the right one. Sasha and I bought a box of pushpins and an enormous map of the world. We hung it on the wall of the unoccupied bedroom—the one we use as a library—so we could trace Dad's voyage: a soft slope up Argentina along the Atlantic coast. Sasha has already read three books about the Pampas region and given me a two-hour summary. It sounds beautiful.

When Jessup finally gets back—with a faint tan and dark circles under his eyes—Erika has the fabulous idea to repaint all the rooms in the house. It's actually something Sasha and I have been thinking about doing for a long time—but ever since the episode last October, we haven't wanted to say anything to our mother about the house.

So the four of us each pick a color—"a happy color," Jessup insists. Those words give me pins and needles in my stomach. I have the horrible feeling we're replacing Dad, covering him up with a tacky coat of paint so he'll disappear forever inside the decrepit walls. I think about it for a long time, but in the end I don't object. It's not Jessup's fault that our house is not our father's anymore. Dad was the one who chose to take off, giving up any say on the color of the walls in the process. Maybe it's finally time for me to take Dad down from his pedestal.

Sasha dithers a hundred times before opting for a particular shade of red. "Coagulated blood," she specifies. Erika can't hide her dismay, but she doesn't actually forbid it, no doubt hoping Sasha will change her mind again. But I know that, for once, there's nothing macabre in Sash's choice. She loves the color because it matches the first orchid I ever planted for her. She's so attached to that plant, she holds a little funeral every time it loses one of its petals.

Our mother, on the other hand, decides on her color right away. She chooses an apple green: "a color that lifts your spirits," she explains. *Or that burns your retinas*, I refrain from saying. I remember the envelope from our father on my birthday, the same Granny Smith green. "It's roaming in some corner of her brain," Sasha whispers in my ear.

Jessup chooses white, clean and neutral, which reminds me of being in his car for the first time, how sterile and cold I found it. His tastes always seem to convey a certain lack of tenderness, of happy memories.

Finally, I choose my favorite blue. The blue of the boat and my bike, of the ribbon around my key and of my favorite sweater—the only one of Dad's that Erika forgot to burn, because it was in my closet and not his. It's the blue of Sasha's eyes the first time I saw her open them as a baby—a color I'll always associate with the most precious thing I have.

We get some pieces of paper, write down the names of all the rooms in the house, and then pull them out of a hat to choose the colors. Erika's room will be red. Our room and the guest room, blue. The living room and bathroom, green. The kitchen, white.

We've made a good start on the job when Jessup stops with his roller in the air, paint trickling down his arm, and proposes moving in before the start of the school year.

"It would be practical!" he says, energetically.

"That's true," Erika reflects cheerfully.

"You'll have to install a shower next to Hannibal Lecter," Sasha retorts, always logical.

Erika looks at me, unable to guess my feelings about this. "What do you think, Phoenix?" she ventures timidly.

Dad has no way of knowing is my first thought. Then I reconsider. Even if he does find out, I don't see why we should feel guilty. Erika's only been with Jessup for five months, but before that, she was alone for eight. We've respected the Year of Isolation mandated by the Unspoken Code of Runaway Fathers. This way Jessup won't have to drive back and forth all the time, seeing as he spends more time here than in his apartment in town. Plus, he's only going to be teaching junior English next year, so I won't be in his class.

"It's a good idea," I conclude.

Jessup lunges to embrace me so suddenly that the canvas protecting the old floor slides under his feet, making him cling to me more forcefully than expected. You'd think I'd just announced the end of world hunger.

Since he's come back, he's been acting strangely. One kind word can provoke a disproportionate surge of affection, a force that makes him seem capable of building a thousand boats with his bare hands. Maybe his time out East was difficult, and he's just happy to see us again.

Anyway, Erika doesn't seem to be complaining. She giggles every time Jessup pounces on her, covering her in wet kisses, acting like Sasha when she plays with Pan, the Baldinis' Samoyed. With Sasha and me, though, he'll do all the right things, but his enthusiasm sometimes rings false. I think even Sasha's noticed that by now; like me, she stays a little on her guard around him. Sometimes he seems like a self-interested child forcing himself to be nice to his grandmother so he'll get a treat. When there's something we want to show him, he doesn't exactly jump out of his chair. First he'll look around for Erika—to see if she's there to be impressed—and then he'll say, "Okay, but quickly, I have things to do." He doesn't always act like that, thankfully, but when he does, we keep our distance. The last thing we want is to doubt his honesty before he's even moved in.

THIRTEEN

A week after Jessup's move-in proposal, with the house still smelling of paint, he sets down his satchel and a battered leather suitcase next to the apothecary chest in the front entrance. Nothing more. There's not even a cardboard box left in the trunk of his car.

"Light travelers have heavy baggage," Sasha says, concerned. "Where's your furniture, your boxes, your knickknacks, your lamps, your plants—"

He cuts her off. "Believe me, there was nothing worth keeping in my hovel." Knowing Jessup's love of cleanliness, the word *hovel* seems extreme. But really, we know almost nothing about that apartment—except that it's the window with yellow shutters above the café, the one on the corner between Sasha's school and the high school.

Once again, he'd rather change the subject.

I notice he hasn't contradicted Sasha about her baggage theory. She doesn't press the matter, because he takes off his glasses and sets about cleaning them with the corner of his T-shirt. I've seen him do this often in class, a sign that he's tired and exasperated. At home, it usually happens at dawn and at dusk, the times when he's at his most melancholy, seeming to carry the misery of the world on his shoulders.

He moves into the house hesitantly, like an animal released into the wild after years in captivity: defenseless, almost frozen, not knowing what to do with so much space and freedom.

First he hangs his coat on a hanger, rather than on the hooks by the front door. Then he looks at the slippers Erika's picked out as if he's never seen slippers in his life, not daring to slide his feet in. His books—just a handful of classics—aren't allowed to mingle with ours in the large bookcase in our living room. They stay in a clear plastic bag under the TV. You'd think Jessup was playing a game of pick-up sticks, afraid to disturb the equilibrium of our environment with the slightest movement. But he's wrong if he thinks we're delicate princesses, living in a palace made of fragile gold leaf. Dad brought us up to be Vikings. *Mud on your boots, dirt under your fingernails, and sweat under your arms*—the three rules we've lived by since we took our first steps.

"I'm worried about Jessup," Sasha confides in me the night he moves in. "You remember what Dad said once?"

"No."

"That you can't trust people who don't have any photos? That the man with no past has no future?"

It's true that Jessup doesn't seem to possess a single family keepsake. Not even a photo stuck in his wallet.

"Don't worry about it. Dad was talking about Nazis," I reassure her. "And Jessup has probably told Erika all about his childhood. We don't tell him everything either, remember."

Sash thinks, then writes something in her notebook, like she's a police chief putting her finger on the crucial piece of evidence in an investigation.

"You—no. *You* don't tell anyone anything," she corrects me. "But I do."

"You tell everyone everything," I tease.

"You pretend not to see it, but you know Jessup's changed," she protests.

I don't deny it. It's impossible not to have noticed. His former energy has vanished along with the fumes from the new paint, leaving a sense of weariness, even depression. As if the summer season of fun and games is coming to an early end, and it's now time to settle into the dull daily routine of autumn.

He settles uneasily into our house over the next few weeks, always seeming irritated somehow. He listens, but less attentively, and cooks, but with less pleasure. On days when Erika's at home, she can still cheer him. But when she's gone, we can't change his mood, no matter what we do.

FOURTEEN

Vanilla is coming over for lunch today. After she called me thirty-four times in three days begging to be invited for a meal with Jessup, I've finally given in. No doubt she's counting on a story to boost her social cred when school starts again next week.

Fortunately, she has no idea how much she annoys him. "You couldn't torture me in a crueler fashion," he replied, when I asked if he minded if I invited her. "Of all the despicable creatures in this world, Miss Paparazzi is by far the worst," he added. He was smirking when he said it, but I got the feeling she truly wasn't the most welcome guest. The date, however, has been set, and I haven't had the courage to call her and cancel.

Vanilla passes through the multicolored rooms, whistling in astonishment. She sits down across from Jessup.

"My mom went through a *colorful* phase after she and my dad split, too," she confesses, touching her scarlet lips. "But, no offense, she didn't go all psychedelic like Ms. Erika!"

Jessup gives her a look I recognize from English class, the look he'd get when our latest essays were so awful he'd clearly rather die than be forced to grade such inanities. I glance over at him, silently begging him to be nice. But instead of his usual slightly mocking look, I see something unfamiliar in his eyes, a strange gleam that frightens me.

"Now I know!" Sasha exclaims, pointing her fork at Vanilla. "You look like that girl in the movie. With the red lipstick. The poster we saw at Bertha's," she says, looking at me.

"*Lolita*," I say. I thought the same thing when she came in the door: the pretty smudge of her mouth, her braids, and her blouse—all looking as innocent as a garter belt. Vanilla is playing the nymphet.

"I couldn't have thought of a better comparison," Jessup adds, sardonically.

"Thanks!" Vanilla replies with a coquettish look.

"That is definitely not a compliment," he shoots back.

She turns redder than her lipstick. I feel the need to defend her.

"The actress is excellent in that movie," I say, candidly.

Jessup practically chokes on his food, a cold and raspy laugh sticking in his throat. I can see Vanilla's confidence collapse like a house of cards in a tsunami.

"You're joking, right?" he coughs. "That bimbo? She's the epitome of vulgar!"

I'm not sure whether he's talking about the actress or Vanilla. Neither is Sash, who is politely avoiding our guest's tearful gaze. I don't understand why Jessup's acting so appallingly. The Mr. Smith I know might say cutting things about students behind their backs, but he would never humiliate someone this way to their face.

I want to tell him, "That's enough," but instead I discreetly kick his chair. Criticizing strangers on the street, fine, but attacking my only social connection in this cruel manner, definitely not. I expect him to hold up his usual index finger in warning, but instead, he strikes back, kicking me in the shin so sharply and forcefully that I wonder if there are knives on the tips of his already pointed shoes. I suppress a cry, keeping my jaw shut. He's not joking. He looks at me like I'm going to be in for a very rough time if I decide to hit his chair again. My voice and my appetite suddenly vanish.

So we go on with this horrible lunch in funereal silence.

Poor Vanilla. Sure, she dolled herself up to get Jessup's attention, but right now she looks as naïve as a little girl who's gotten into her mother's makeup. She wasn't trying to seduce him or anything. She just wanted a smile and a wink, maybe a kiss on the cheek—that would have been enough for her to brag about all year.

After we take our dishes to the kitchen, Vanilla insists on washing off her lipstick. I'm confused. I don't know how to explain to her what just happened. Jessup can be harsh, sure, but he's never acted this way. A transformation like that can't be all Vanilla's doing.

Sasha and I try to cheer her up, but she heads for the door, joking bitterly about "escaping the lair of the devil." When she leaves, her morale is lower than the soles of her ballerina flats.

I send Sasha out to water the plants so I can talk to Jessup. I don't want to alarm her over a little kick, which I'm sure he'll fall over himself apologizing for.

"Look, you hurt me," I say, showing him the mark on my leg and pouting in exaggerated pain.

The other day, Sash got a kiss on her finger for

a much lesser injury. I'm not even asking for that. A bandage and a kind word will be enough.

"That will teach you," he says, without an ounce of humor. "Always challenging my authority."

No apology, then. No bandage.

"I'm not your friend," he adds sternly.

I nod, speechless.

Jessup exhales, his hands firmly planted on his hips. He comes closer to me. It's silly, but I step back.

"You can count yourself lucky there's only one mark on your leg, given how many times you've been insolent," he says. "I knew I should have been firm from the start. And in the future, find some friends who are your equals in intelligence! I don't want to see *that* in my house again, okay?"

He doesn't wait for a response, just turns and quietly goes back to the living room.

I don't want to see *that*? Does he mean Vanilla? My heart feels like it's beating in my temples, or in my ears. I stand there in the kitchen for a long moment, dizzy. I clean up the dishes as well as I can making the least noise possible, as if Jessup's prohibition of *that* applies equally to the clinking of silverware or the sight of a poorly rinsed plate.

"We have a dishwasher," Sasha says from behind me. "Why are you scrubbing so hard? What's wrong?"

Her eyes have that strange glassiness they get when she's on the edge of a panic attack.

"Help me dry," I say quickly.

"You're almost as bizarre as Jessup. Did he tell you off? Did you get mad at him?"

To distract her, I stick my finger in the leftover asparagus mousse and dab it on her nose. She bursts out laughing and rubs her face with the tea towel. I exhale, but the tension is still there inside me.

"You two conspiring?" Jessup asks, poking his head through the partially open door. I jump, then laugh nervously. The atmosphere is different all of a sudden, as if something heavy and opaque has settled on us. I barely have time to think before Sasha grabs an enormous glob of mousse and heads for Jessup. My heart races as I stand there listening to them screaming and laughing, my hands gripping the edge of the sink. I've lost control of my body. I can't move. I hear the echo of his threat: *You can count yourself lucky there's only one mark on your leg.* But Jessup's laughter is so loud and genuine it snaps me out of my daze, forcing me to lock that strange pronouncement away by itself somewhere, separate from the rest of me.

"Phoenix! Help me!" he cries, running through the hall at full throttle. Sasha follows with the mousse still in her hand.

I smile, feeling suddenly lighter.

Jessup wasn't thinking when he said that. He obviously feels bad about what he did. He's never gotten seriously angry with us. He just didn't know how to handle the situation. Or he was just in a bad mood. It happens to everyone.

His threat now as small as a microscopic bacterium swimming in my stomach, I run to join them.

FIFTEEN

It's six-thirty and Sasha is looking for her white skirt in the laundry hamper. Every year she performs the same scene. We get our things ready the night before and then, at the last minute, she picks a different outfit. This morning, with Erika away on another trip, Jessup is doing his best to hurry her along.

"The one with the parrot on the back pocket," she tells him as he checks the closet for the third time. "I was wearing it that day you told Phoenix she had to choose an extracurricular activity this year. I suggested theater but she said no. Because of *Marlon*, if you want my opinion."

It's too early for me to get involved in a conversation this stressful, especially if *Marlon* is going to be brought into it for no reason. Getting up this morning was hard. It always is before nine o'clock, unless it's to go fishing.

"Sasha, I don't want to be late because of a parakeet skirt," Jessup says, getting impatient. "Why don't you wear what Phoenix put out? What difference does it make?"

My sister has her beliefs. Trying to dislodge them is like attempting to dig a hole in concrete with a plastic spoon. According to her, your first-day outfit determines who you'll be for the rest of the year. If you make your choice lightly, you might as well go to school naked.

"Jessup, if you're looking for a parakeet, you'll never find my skirt, because it's a *parrot*. They have a shorter tail, and macaws—"

"Sash, wear something else, please," I say.

I don't want her to irritate him any more.

She shrugs, grabbing the unwanted skirt and heading to the bathroom.

"I'll hold you responsible if I end up the laughing-stock of the playground!" she shouts, slamming the door.

She's acting so immature that I burst out laughing.

I'm still in my pajamas in front of my cereal bowl when Jessup comes into the kitchen, radiating impatience, jangling his keys like a baby with a rattle. We have plenty of time, I just have to put on a shirt and jeans, but he doesn't seem to be of the same mind.

"Phoenix!" he hisses between his teeth.

No need to say more; I know this military tone. I've

heard it a lot in the last few days. Ever since the incident with Vanilla, it seems like everything I do displeases him. I hurriedly try to gulp the rest of the chocolatey milk. But just before I reach the sink, I trip and the bowl slips from my hands. The milk splatters on Jessup's pants before spreading across the floor, and the bowl shatters at his feet. Instead of grabbing a sponge to clean up, I freeze. A bad feeling crawls through my intestines. Jessup closes his eyes, no doubt thinking about the time he's going to lose changing his pants. I wait for his rebuke, ready to apologize.

Silence.

In a flash, his hand makes contact with my cheek, or maybe it's his fist, because it's as forceful as a hammer blow. My head snaps back and I hit my cheekbone against the frame of the open window. Pain enflames my face, and my heart is beating so fast that it hurts my chest. I have to stop myself from laughing because it's so absurd, comical even. He just slipped, I tell myself, like that time we were painting the house—he's still not used to this floor, that dangerous spot where our mother polishes her shoes. He can't have done it on purpose.

But when I lift my burning face, I see no glimmer in Jessup's eyes. Only disgust, and something as dangerous as a hungry wolf.

"That will teach you," he declares, his jaw tight.

That will teach you. The same words again. So that kick last week really *was* a warning.

I've never been slapped before. I've never even been spanked. Erika says that children aren't horses, that it's useless to hit them when you can speak to them instead.

Panicking all of a sudden, I crouch down to pick up the pottery shards. My hands are quivering, inches from Jessup's shoes, which are drowning in a puddle of milk. Then he kneels down and helps me pick up the pieces, his hands strong and assured. I watch the sleeves of his jacket brushing along the damp floor, getting stained as he wipes his fingers, those same fingers that were on my cheek seconds before. I hear the slap, again and again.

"Come on, don't look so upset," he says gently. Suddenly his hot breath is burning the top of my head and he deposits a kiss before leaving. What does he think? A kind gesture and I'll forget?

I carefully count his thirteen quick steps up the stairs before I stand, shaky, my mind as cloudy as the sky before a storm. I'm on the edge of a cliff, suffocating, but not with tears. I'm much too furious to cry. I'm so angry at myself I can't breathe. I'm angry for being silent, for putting up with his mood swings, his reproaches, his punishments. I've tried all week to avoid being alone with him. To be honest, he's starting to terrify me.

I can't help it: every particle of air I struggle to

breathe is dense with fear, a fear that weakens me. Instead of rising above Jessup's rage, I bury myself under it. I'm the victim in a horror movie, the one who goes into the cave without a light. The one who dies first.

I'm a coward and it makes me sick. I feel like I'm five years old again, imagining a branch outside my window is a clawed hand, about to grab me, and not even daring to call Dad because I'm so paralyzed with fear. Then, I was naïve enough to think a heavy blanket could protect me from an imaginary monster. But now, I know I have to face a stepfather who's very real.

This is the last time, I think, chasing away the doubts and fear. I'll tell Erika everything.

I avoid touching my sore cheek because Sasha is there, ready to go, carrying Jessup's satchel.

She doesn't have to know.

"You're bleeding! What did you do?" she asks, panicking, reaching for my cheek. I catch her fingers, her skin so translucent you can see her veins. She lets out a little cry.

"She tried to kiss the window," Jessup answers, coming out of nowhere. He gives me a complicit wink.

I confirm this story with a sheepish look, then go upstairs to quickly get dressed.

That makes twice that I've hidden the truth about

Jessup from my sister. I'm lucky, she won't interrogate me today. She's too preoccupied with the idea of starting grade four to notice my legs like jelly and my eyes filled with terror.

SIXTEEN

In the still-empty school halls, I replay this morning's scene.

I'll never call him Jessup again, I mutter. From now on it will be Mr. Smith, like before. He's lost the privilege of being called by his first name. *Mr. Smith is violent*, I repeat, until the words seem incoherent and meaningless. Like Mary Poppins's *supercalifragilisticexpialidocious*, only with the opposite effect. A harmful mantra.

"Friday!" I'd recognize the voice even underwater.

Marlon.

I've never been so happy to see his smile, his face brimming with memories of his holiday. He tugs on his backpack straps, looking flustered. I turn my face so he won't notice anything unusual.

"I know, it's Monday," he says. "But I couldn't wait."

He crouches down and rummages through his bag, one knee on the ground. Then he hands me a rectangular shape wrapped in newspaper. It's heavy. I try to ignore the pain stinging my cheek as I calculate the density of the object.

"A personal gift," he says with a wink.

Mr. Smith's wink comes back to me, like the chorus of some catchy but terrible song.

"Wow! Did you get attacked by a tourist?"

I tense and look at the floor. His ski-instructor tan and adorable bedhead had almost distracted me from thinking about it.

"I slipped this morning."

"Ouch!" he exclaims.

Before I can stop him, his fingers graze the double mark left by the window frame, his eyes inspecting the wound like a surgeon. I hold my breath.

"Aren't you going to open it?" he asks, tapping the object in my sweaty hands, which are glued to the newspaper.

I can't. Not in the hall. I don't want to attract more attention. The first students are already here, and my opening a package from Marlon would get us on the front page of Vanilla's blog. Even if it would be a nice distraction, I'd rather not be the focal point of gossip on the first day of school. My head is very much elsewhere.

I need space to think of the best way to tell Erika about *the thing*.

"I'll open it at home."

"In case it's atrociously ugly," he guesses.

I shake my head no, firmly. It could be a bag of chips and I'd think it was wonderful, unexpected but wonderful. I'm about to explain when he adds:

"Well, it's cool not to break my heart in public. But if you hate it, tell me—I'd rather you be honest."

His meadow-green eyes inspect me again. He's serious and, I have to admit, he looks disarmingly sincere.

"Shit! I have training in two minutes," he says, looking at his watch. "I never notice time passing when I'm with you. You'll let me know about the present, hey?"

I nod, then whisper a "thank you," but he's already at the end of the hall, adjusting his bag on his shoulder. I wait for him to turn back and look at me, which he does, twice. Pretending to concentrate on my schedule, I conceal my smile, tamp down my desire to see him again as soon as possible, and place his gift behind the stack of new textbooks.

"What did Baldini want from you?" Vanilla inquires, putting her arm around my shoulder.

"Hello to you too," I say, pulling away.

"You didn't tell him about Dean and the books, I hope?"

"Never!" I say, hurt that she would doubt me. I can keep a secret.

"Relax, I know you're an angel! Not like your wicked stepfather, right?"

For once Vanilla and I have the same thing on our minds. I laugh timidly, still glancing behind me in case Mr. Smith appears as swiftly as a stitch in the side. He's always there when you're not expecting him.

"Please don't say you're sorry again!" she exclaims, as if she's read my thoughts. "I got your thousand and one messages. I'm not mad at you, you have nothing to apologize for. Honestly, it's you I feel bad for."

She feels bad for me? Could she ... No, I can't let myself panic. There's no way she could know. She wasn't there in the kitchen this morning. I have to stay rational.

"Smith has a fucked up sense of humor!" Vanilla explains.

I nod quickly. She's talking about the Lolita Incident, it's all good. My cold sweat evaporates as quickly as it appeared.

"Come on, tell me about your fight! Did the Antichrist

bang up your cheek with his forked tail, or was it Baldini getting rough? What did he want from you, anyway?"

Her words bore into my stomach. I fake a laugh before leaving her in front of her class, relieved that I don't have to see her again until lunch. She'll have dug her claws into some more interesting prey by then.

Meanwhile, I head to biology class. The lab smells like formaldehyde and sulfur, just what I need to take my mind off things. Unfortunately, there's no escaping Mr. Smith today. When he's not in my head, he's in the halls. I cross paths with him four times and each time he greets me like I've just handed him the winning ticket in the lottery, obliging me to do the same. A few other students smile at me enviously and I feel sick. I'm the only one who knows of the existence of the Mr. Smith Paradox: on one side, the charming teacher, adored by all; on the other, the authoritarian stepfather, lurking in our house with violence in his hands and humiliation on his tongue. And I'm the only one who can find out which of the two is the real one.

SEVENTEEN

On Friday night, Sasha and I are watching the sun set when our mother appears. She races out of the car and across the beige gravel in front of the house, her ankles wobbling on her high heels and a jumble of files under her arm. She looks so agitated that for a second I think she's been in an accident. But the car shows no traces of a crash.

"My god, Phoenix, what did you do to yourself now?" she asks.

I didn't think she'd even notice my cheek. Ignoring her irritation, I'm about to hug her when she adds:

"Were you out climbing in the forest again? Maybe it's time to stop playing the wildling and act like a young lady, don't you think?"

Right. Put on a skirt, some sandals, a flowery blouse,

some nail polish—in summary, look like Vanilla. But I stifle my annoyance at her lectures on femininity. She's giving me the chance to tell her the truth on a silver platter.

"I didn't do this climb—"

"You went to school like that?" she interrupts.

"Yes," I reply, taken aback. What was I supposed to do—put on my spare face?

"In this moth-eaten sweater? I hope you're kidding. Look at the collar!"

I'm too stunned to reply. Here I thought my mother was concerned about the scrape on my cheek when all she cares about are the holes in my sweater. The window of trust has already shut. Anyway, she's clearly not here to see us. If she just about twisted her ankle in her haste to get home, it was for Mr. Smith, who's just come out on the porch with his arms open wide.

She rushes toward him, as eager as Sasha running off to look up a word in the dictionary, and they kiss with a repugnant ardor. You'd think it was the reunion of two lovers torn apart by war in a melodramatic movie.

"You're louder than Niagara Falls!" Sash comments, sticking her fingers in her ears.

As the lovebirds' laughter rings out, it occurs to me that it's going to be hard to break it to our mother that my former English teacher might not be the kind of man she wants to grow old with. It's not that I won't be prepared. I've practiced my speech as rigorously as an orator in the Agora in ancient Athens, repeating it day and night. I know I'll have to be subtle, watching for the next opportunity and seizing it. But the one thing I hadn't planned on was that Mr. Smith would go back to being the way he was before—in the days of roses, waffles, and *Alice in Wonderland*'s White Rabbit.

At dinner he tells us anecdotes about his new students. He's all charm. Then he solicitously lets each of us speak, without interrupting, making attentive comments—a big contrast to his apathetic shrugging of the last few weeks. I don't recognize the man who slapped me. Once more he's the kind, devoted teacher everyone adores. His expression is bright again, as if his features have been lit up, yesterday's blur erased. He's warm and spontaneous and so engaging with me that I feel guilty for wanting to crucify him so quickly. I'm not sure I know who I'm dealing with anymore. Maybe Mr. Smith has simply gone through a difficult time that he hasn't been able to talk about with us. If that's the case, I understand. I wasn't the easiest person to love either, after Dad left.

The four of us have such a good time over the weekend that the speech I prepared becomes muddled, with only hesitant fragments left. The air around us has lightened, like school binders emptied over the holidays. Obviously the slap and the threats are still there, idling in a corner of my brain. But doubt has settled at the base of my throat, wilting my arguments like Dad's petunias. *It was just a passing mood. We'll start from scratch*, I tell myself. If Jessup needs Erika in order to be a better person, just like she needs him, I have to give them a second chance. It would be selfish of me to ruin their efforts.

I'll forgive him.

Sasha and I barely hear the knock on the door of our room. Jessup usually enters abruptly, with no consideration for our privacy.

It's Erika. She waits in the hallway for authorization to come in.

"Kitten, could you help Jessup with the popcorn machine, please?" she asks Sasha, once we've invited her in.

Sweet words from her are too uncommon to ignore, so Sash hurtles downstairs, shouting about never, ever touching the blue button. I close my math textbook and put the cap on my pen, but I stay sitting at my desk; I'm embarrassed to find myself alone with Erika. *If anyone here objects to this union, speak now or forever hold your peace*, I think. If I don't tell her now, there won't be another chance. I make a decision. I will, once and for all,

sweep aside my last doubts about Jessup. I'm determined
to leave our family in peace, to make us happy, even.

"We need to talk," Erika announces, advancing
awkwardly on the thick carpet.

My mother is an intimidating woman, seldom
intimidated. Still, she sits on the edge of my bed, hands
on her knees like a studious little girl, scrutinizing the
room nervously. She wets her lips a few times, revealing
her anxiety—so different from Sasha's because it's much
rarer.

"I understand this situation is difficult for you," she
says, her eyes closed.

Taken aback, I press the buttons on my calculator,
contemplating the zeros lined up like ballet dancers. Our
mother has never given us life lessons before, or even
spoken to us with any reflection or depth. She's always
been content with the superficial, never there for the
essential. Dad took charge of our real education, the
difficult conversations about heartache, love, death, birth
control, and all the other important things. "Knowledge
of the heart," he called it.

"A difficult situation ... because of your father, his ...
his departure ..."

She leaves out her share of the responsibility, as
usual. Our father might have sailed off last year, but
she's been sailing in the distance forever.

I swing my legs under the desk so I'm no longer facing her, letting my hair slide along my cheek to hide my profile. I'm hoping, cruelly, to stop her from continuing this pitiful attempt at a heart-to-heart. It's unbearable, coming so badly and so late.

"But I don't think that's a good reason to give Jessup a hard time," she continues, suddenly icy.

I look at her, my mouth hanging open, speechless. What is she talking about?

She lengthens her neck and her face takes on that imperious expression that's so typical of her. Untouchable. Here I was thinking she wanted to talk about my feelings, about the postcards, or the greenhouse. How naïve! I'd even been considering the possibility that she was worried about Sash, that she would tell me to stop encouraging her false hope that Dad will come back. Just about every scenario crossed my mind except this one.

She rises slowly and approaches me with gravity, as if she's about to tell me the meaning of life.

"He told me that you two argued."

"Argued?" I repeat, with a somber scowl.

She knits her eyebrows. Obviously that wasn't the reaction she expected.

"Yes, argued," she insists drily. "You think he doesn't tell me what's going on here when I'm away? Jessup worries a lot about you. He said that you started off the year very badly, that you spoke to him rudely, that you've been coming in late and abandoning Sasha completely. I know you're more withdrawn, more ... irritable lately. But since when do you not care about your little sister?" She loses her temper on the last words, stunning even herself with their force.

How dare she presume to know what I care about? She barely knows me! That stupid question—I'm speechless. Nothing could hurt me more than being accused of abandoning Sasha. Erika knows it, too; that's exactly the spot where she wanted to pierce me. Straight through the heart.

"I'm very disappointed, Phoenix. This isn't the way I raised you," she adds, all regretful.

I'm as rigid and blank as a cadaver. I try to remember how to breathe. The slap, the lies, the false accusations, the supposed teen angst, Sasha ... how much more blame can I endure? I'm furious. My mouth opens suddenly, like it's being pulled by an invisible thread, letting loose a rage I've held in far too long.

"Are you kidding me? *You're* the one who's disappointed? Because you think *you* raised us?"

I don't have time to regret my words before I feel the slap. It's less painful than Jessup's, but even more difficult to bear. I turn away so I don't have to see the remorseful look on her face. Sash is standing in the middle of the hall, shaking, her hands over her mouth. I motion to her to get lost, but she advances, like the last samurai on a ruined battlefield.

"Wh ... why?" she asks, her eyes shining with tears. It's not Erika she's asking, it's me.

"I deserved it. I was very rude to her," I say. I'm not sure where the voice comes from.

Sasha shakes her head and then flings herself at me with full force, her face pressing into my side, her nails digging into my back. *Liar*, she repeats over and over.

Erika steps back, crossing her arms over her chest, as if seeing us has sent shivers down her spine. Or maybe she's just trying to comfort herself.

If our mother would say just one sentence, just one word ... if she'd ask for an explanation instead of judging me, I would put my arms around her. I'd tell her I'm not her enemy. That she's our only family now, that she needs to believe in me, in us. If I could trust Erika, we could be like a normal daughter and mother. I'd ask her to sit down again, to listen to me, and she'd believe me. She'd get rid of Mr. Smith and we'd embrace each other, the three of us. There would be no need for grand declarations; we'd just know that we're family. But that's not reality. The lies of a stranger have come to destroy me, reduced me to the level of Dad's incinerated things. Erika retreats from the room as if it were on fire. I guess I'm not worth the trouble of saving, either.

Sash sits by the bedroom window, which is what she does when she's worried about something but doesn't have the energy for a panic attack. She got into the habit after Dad left, as if the answers to all her questions would miraculously bloom from the smooth, calm surface of the lake.

I wait for the moon to appear above the beech trees before interrupting her thoughts. I don't turn on the light, not wanting to disturb the twilight's soothing glow. I just grab the flashlight under Sasha's pillow and shine it at her.

"Did you put your pajamas on backwards to scare monsters away?"

She laughs and I feel all my muscles relax, like the feeling when I take off my roller skates. I'm as light as a dandelion seed floating above the ground. I help her put on her top the right way, pausing to tickle her belly until she rolls on the floor, begging me to stop, tears of laughter in the corners of her eyes. But once she calms down, Sash dives back into her unfathomable thoughts, looking out the window again.

"Do you want to see something amazing?" I say.

She nods, coming back to reality but still pensive. I shut the door—as if I could shut out bad thoughts along with it—and then pull out the newspaper-wrapped package from under my bed. Sasha rushes to my side, captivated. She curls up against my waist and I settle into her embrace. I need consoling as much as she does. I want to think about other things, and her wildflower smell helps distract me.

We study Marlon's wooden box. It's obviously made by hand: the lid is too big and it creaks when it opens because the hinges weren't placed right. Still, the top is beautifully carved: two fish with their fins crossed, surrounded by a garland. It's like the coat of arms of a royal family. Sasha caresses the object as if it were a magical creature, just as I did when I first unwrapped it and discovered Marlon's hidden talents.

"This is it, the special box for our *Eupholus bennetti*," she announces triumphantly.

The most precious beetle in our collection, the bright-blue one Dad brought us from Papua New Guinea. It deserves a mausoleum all to itself, and Sasha's right, the box is perfect.

"Was there something inside?" she mumbles, yawning. She's still nosy, in spite of her tiredness, and that cheers me up. Her good humor is returning, little by little. I give her a hug and then slide the little spiral notebook into her hands.

I've already read it forty-nine times.

With a sleepy smile, Sash reads the words on the cover, laminated with scotch tape. *"Phoenix the Hero."*

I turn the pages as she snores, her little sleeping body resting against mine, soft as a jellyfish.

For the fiftieth time, I marvel at the skill of the pen drawings, black and precise. They remind me of Anders Nilsen, an illustrator Dad always said was a genius. The comic-strip panels tell the story of a girl with long hair like mine who fights scary, deformed mutants, tossing off deadly glares and icy quips. On my eighth read, I realized that Marlon had managed to incorporate a quotation on every page from one of the books recommended by Dean, including *The Great Gatsby*. Because the notebook is small, I can carry it in my pocket, protected by a freezer bag, fearing nothing. Even if it's the least effective talisman ever, I can't bear to part with it. It comforts me.

The next morning, before Erika leaves for her longest trip yet, I get the feeling that a little part of her wishes she could do or say something more. She bites her thumb nervously, which is what she does when she's searching for words. But she doesn't soften, and she doesn't hug us goodbye. She slams the car door and starts the ignition.

We watch the car sink into the woods until she's just a colored dot among the others on the edge of the lake.

Now we're alone again with Smith—who no longer deserves to be called *father* or even *mister*. The stranger has taken over our home.

EIGHTEEN

The drama club meets every Wednesday after school at the Baldinis' place. I tag along with Sasha since I don't want to be alone at home with Smith. I don't have to do anything more than breathe in order to irritate him.

We meet Ivan and Bertha in the school parking lot. They're smoking, leaning against a tree, like two cowboys in an old Western. The spicy aroma of their smoke curls is familiar. If I close my eyes, I can see our father with a clove cigarette between his fingers. We got another postcard from him yesterday, but instead of comforting me, each one makes me angrier that he's not here.

Marlon, Prudence, and Dean join us and we climb into Bertie's huge van, which smells like sleet and plastic. There are crumpled papers and open cookie packages on the dashboard. A few empty cans roll at our feet. Crumbs of all sorts have infiltrated the grooves in the seats. A car should always carry traces of its past adventures, like this one, I think. Not like Smith's spotless four-star hotel on wheels.

Prudence switches on the radio and turns up the volume. "It's as loud as a nightclub in here!" Sasha yells happily over the music. I can feel the bass all the way through my stomach. The planet hanging from the rearview mirror swings in rhythm to an old Cat Stevens hit, and everyone sings along at the top of their lungs. I know the song, but I don't sing. Dean nudges me repeatedly, but I don't want to. I don't feel like I belong to their clan. There's too much noise, too much life, too much joy: I feel like a foreigner. I slept badly. I'm exhausted. It's like I'm wearing headphones with another kind of music playing, something sadder and wearier. Maybe the wicked stepfather's bad mood is contagious.

The Baldinis live a few trees down from the sawmill, in a long, flat house that looks like a plank of wood. The view of the lake is stunning. It stretches so far that I can see our house, which looks ridiculously small, like a troglodyte's cave engulfed by the vast forest.

"When the sky is clear, we can see you on your boat," Marlon says.

"Didn't you tell me it's been ten days since you've spotted them?" Dean asks him.

Marlon nods. His ears have turned red. So he wasn't lying when he said he noticed me.

"It's too cold right now," I explain before anyone asks.

Even if the sky had been clear and the temperature warm, Marlon wouldn't have seen the boat. Smith has forbidden me to use it because I forgot to empty the dishwasher and do my chemistry exercises once last week. And Sasha isn't allowed to use the boat alone. At least autumn is short here; winter will come soon to spread its layer of ice on the lake, making boating impossible.

"If it freezes solid, you'll be able to see us skating," Sasha says.

I doubt the wicked stepfather will let us do anything that fun, but I let her believe it.

"That would be great! We could even join you, right, Marco?" says Dean.

"You bet, Polo!" Marlon replies. They hold hands and pretend to be a pair of figure skaters, pirouetting around us.

"She smiles, at last!" Dean exclaims, applauding me.

We've barely been sitting for two minutes in front of the crackling fireplace when Prudence hands us each a cup of hot chocolate. I look around at the old-fashioned décor. With the antique furniture, doilies, and curios, it looks like a grandmother's house. Still, it's cozier than our place. I especially like all the mismatched plants overrunning their living room. I think rooms have more heart when they're disorderly. Smith's rearrangements have made our home a drab and sterile place, devoid of flowers or dust. A home in his own image.

I slip out after the first hour of theater talk and play outside with Marlon's dog, Pan, until my fingers are so stiff with cold I can't throw him the tennis ball.

"You'll catch a cold," Marlon says, standing in the entrance of a French door that leads to a bedroom.

He spreads his arms, as if to add, *If that's what you want.* I join him, my legs as rigid as stalagmites.

I see his leather jacket and his scooter helmet tossed in the corner of what must be his room. It looks like an aquarium—narrow, blue, and luminous. I take off my boots so my damp soles won't leave marks on the carpet. I feel awkward. The hole in my worn-out sock doesn't help matters. But he doesn't seem to care, too busy trying to hide his bathing suit, which is hanging to dry on the door of his closet. There are board games and stacks of sketchbooks piled up inside. But what draws my attention is a photo of an arctic-blond man—the spitting image of Marlon, though older, and even more handsome.

Could this be the famous Norwegian?

"That's my biological dad, Espen Danielsen. The Norwegian," he says, as if I had asked the question out loud.

His warm breath on my cheek feels like an invisible film, as strong as a spider's web.

"You were adopted?" I ask.

"Hmm, no, I wish."

With no further explanation, he picks up the frame and slides to the floor, his head resting against the bed.

"I only keep this photo to remind myself of what I can never let myself become," he says, his voice cracking.

I don't know what to say. I wasn't expecting a confession. But it would be cold of me to do nothing. So I sit down beside him, quickly, almost like a reflex, ready to listen. He pulls his knees to his chest, clears his throat, and continues.

"Mom and I lived with him in Oslo then. We stayed there until I was ... fourteen. As you can probably guess, he hit my mom the whole time."

I couldn't guess that, no. How could you guess that anyone could hit Prudence? It would be like someone raising their hand to Sasha. I shiver, feeling like I'm falling into emptiness.

Marlon lets out a sudden, short sigh, like a gust of air sweeping away my thoughts.

"I don't know where I got the strength that night. I pushed him onto the road before I knew what I was doing. By the time I saw the car coming, it was too late. He died instantly," he says in a low voice.

His last sentence weighs so heavily—I feel it in the silence that submerges the room. I think of something I read somewhere: *The most precious intimacy is to not need to speak.* So I keep them to myself, all the obvious phrases like *I understand. That's awful. I'm so sorry.* I can't respond to his bravery with everyday words that everyone uses. I'd have to invent a new language to match the level of trust he's given me.

Marlon watches me patiently out of the corner of his eye. My brain feels as empty as a plastic bag floating in the wind.

A spider wanders between the cracks in the closet. I feel even tinier than it is.

"You're not going to say anything? Are you scared of me now?" he asks sadly.

"No, not at all."

I look him in the eyes so he understands. A lot of feelings are going through me, but none of them is fear.

"It was an accident," I say, with conviction.

He rests his head on my shoulder, a bit awkwardly. The position is uncomfortable and he's hurting me a bit, but I'll stay this way as long as he needs me to. Forever, if necessary.

"So, Friday, now that you know, can we pretend I never said anything?" he implores me gently.

"You never said what?" I whisper, smiling.

He sits up slowly and kisses my cheek, as light as a flea jumping. I don't know why, but Annabelle Frost's face appears in my head, taunting me. *He would have given* me *a real kiss*, she brags.

Marlon studies me, looking disappointed. Or maybe I'm the one who's disappointed.

"You want to tell me anything?"

"No. Well, yes. I forgot to thank you for the gifts. They're beautiful," I murmur.

My words sound cool, but I mean them sincerely.

"Ivan told me that if you loved the box, you would fill it right away," Marlon declares, impishly.

I know what he means. It's like when you run right outside to try a new bicycle. Or you read a book until you know certain pages by heart.

"So?" he says.

"We're using it to keep the nicest beetle in our collection."

He bursts out laughing. Suddenly, there's no more trace of his confession on his face. His expression is bright and pure, all thoughts of the Norwegian gone.

"You'll show me the beetle one of these days?" he asks, suddenly serious.

"If you want me to."

"I really, really want you to."

It's time to go home.

Prudence wraps up three pieces of hazelnut cake, "For your dessert tonight," she says. I think Sasha has stopped breathing, she's so touched by the gesture. It's been a long time since anyone has wrapped something in tinfoil for us.

NINETEEN

I look at the clock in the front entrance instinctively. It's six forty-nine. We're back early; the wicked stepfather will be pleased with us. No doubt we'll have earned his homemade iced tea, his favorite reward of the moment. You'd think we were seals doing pirouettes for a sardine.

The days of Black Forest cake and laughter seem so far away.

"Am I imagining things or do you stink of cigarettes?" he accuses, suddenly facing us in the hall with his arms crossed over his apron.

Sash sniffs her sweater and scarf, then shrugs, passing by without looking him in the face. He catches her by the edge of her coat. I freeze. His other hand is on his hip and he looks like an airport security guard, waiting for the slightest transgression to set off the *beep* of his alarm.

"It's no big deal. Ivan and Bertha smoked all afternoon," I say, as nonchalantly as possible.

Smith takes a step backward, his eyes wide, looking like I just told him the world was ending.

"No big deal? You think it's no big deal to be seventeen years old and reek of smoke?" he exclaims, laughing humorlessly. "Even worse, you think it's no big deal to leave an eight-year-old girl in a smokehouse?"

I shake my head and retreat. I don't want to spoil this good day by annoying him further.

"Your mother warned you that Ivan and Bertie are toxic!"

Erika never said anything of the sort. She simply suggested that we avoid talking about politics and the environment with them, which we did.

Strangely, the wicked stepfather decides to leave us alone.

But it goes without saying that we won't have iced tea tonight.

It's barely eight-thirty when he turns off the TV. There's an idea in the back of his mind; I recognize that menacing glint at the edge of his irises.

"Go up to your room. I'll be there soon," he orders.

We don't even try to discuss, although I wonder what

he'll want from us once we're up there. He usually checks our homework earlier in the evening, in Dad's old office. Maybe we've earned a lecture about the harmful effects of tobacco on children.

On the staircase, Sash giggles as she mimics Smith and his sergeant-major attitude. I force myself to join in, but I'm worried by the murmurs of irritation coming from the living room. A few minutes pass before he turns up in our room, not knocking, his sleeves rolled up like he's a mechanic about to get his hands dirty.

"There are two types of people I detest above all: the weak and recruiters," he says.

"Like army recruiters?" Sasha asks, confused.

"Like Big Bertha," he fumes, "who couldn't care less about your health. And your sister, who follows her like an idiot!"

Here we go, another tirade against Bertie. Sasha and I turn back to our homework, pretending to listen to him. With the back of his hand, the wicked stepfather sends my history book flying to the other side of the room.

"Come on, get up, inspection!" he proclaims proudly. "Empty all your drawers, now!"

Sasha bursts out laughing. It's the first time she's seen him this way, like a storm about to crack the earth. Not me.

He glares at her with such an icy look that it gives me shivers. She doesn't notice, so I pinch her bum firmly. Judging by how fast she turns serious, I must look frightened. "It's okay," I tell her quietly before getting up.

"I'm not going to repeat myself!" he shouts.

I comply.

He stands behind me as I pull out our jeans, our shirts, our shorts, one by one, unfolding them carefully so he can see I'm not hiding any cigarettes. He runs his hands inside the empty drawers, checking every corner with the precision of a bomb-disposal expert.

Sasha hasn't budged an inch on my bed. She's staring at me, her mouth hanging open, and I can hear her breaths becoming shallow and shaky. I smile, hoping to calm her before the panic attack becomes inevitable.

"Good. Now this one," the wicked stepfather orders, nodding his head.

"That's just our underwear," I murmur, embarrassed.

"And?"

"It's private!" Sasha cries.

He takes off his glasses and cleans them with his sweater, closing his eyes.

"Nothing is private in a family. Open it."

"Come on, this is ridiculous, I don't smoke," I protest, smiling nervously.

"Phoenix, I swear to you, if I have to open it myself, I'm not going to be happy."

His voice is unexpectedly calm. My muscles tense. The memory of his threat comes back to me like a boomerang. But I can't show him our underwear.

It's humiliating.

His eyes dart back and forth from the dresser to my face, more and more insistent. He scratches his head like a dog, paw behind the ear, exasperated and enraged. I can hear my heart racing in my chest.

"Please, Jessup, you know I don't smoke," I repeat softly.

It happened too fast.

I must have closed my eyes, because I didn't see anything coming. All I know is that the blows rained down, no kind gesture this time to temper their brutality. Now I'm on the ground, curled up, short of breath, with a strange nausea burning my entrails. I feel my lungs buzzing, like a plane about to crash. Sasha is crying out insults. The door closes behind the wicked stepfather— metamorphosed into his true self—with such a racket that the frame on the wall containing our *Lucanus cervus* falls and breaks against the desk. The poor beetle is decapitated, its mandibles broken.

Sash is standing—safe and sound, I tell myself, relieved. But she's shaking, her face wet. She runs her hands all over me. I start to feel my body again under her fingers, which seem sharp as an animal's claws on my sore flesh.

"I'm fine, it's okay," I say in a dull voice, painfully extracting myself from her grasp.

I hold on to the dresser, unstable, trying to regain my balance. I'm folded in half; my sides feel like they've gone through a shredder. The desk chair is tipped over, Marlon's box is broken, and a few books are scattered at my feet.

The storm reappears suddenly in the room, violently, grabbing my pajamas, my pillow, and my backpack as quick as a shoplifter. I'm paralyzed by a million things, mostly fear.

"As of tonight, you sleep in *your* room!" he orders, mechanically.

"No, no, no!" roars Sasha, grabbing the pillow. He pulls it back easily and without emotion, stroking her hair and whispering something soothing like "Calm down, little kitten." This produces the inverse effect: a hailstorm of insults.

I'm not listening anymore.

My arms dangling, in a daze, I watch them as if they're people I don't know. And it's true, I don't recognize anyone in this moment. Everything is strange. As if I weren't even certain of being myself, Phoenix Cotton. As if this has just happened to someone else—in a movie, maybe. All that kicking, all that violence; it's impossible that it really happened. Here. With Sasha watching.

She holds my arm as I keep walking forward. If I stop, I'll collapse.

I go with this man—wearing his regular face again— into this room that's not mine. I sit on this bed, my hands on these knees, looking at the dozens of postcards pinned to the wall without really seeing them. The door closes and I'm alone, cloistered in another space-time, where nothing more can happen to me. I hear muffled voices and then the harrowing sobs of a little girl piercing the walls, but I can't go to her. I'm too hurt or too scared to do or say anything, or even to think. I don't know anymore. I don't know anymore if I'm alive.

When I wake up, Sasha's face is above mine. A beam of light makes the dust particles sparkle around us, those few that have resisted the vacuum's repeated assaults. I look for my bedside table on my right, but it's disappeared. That's strange, because on my left is a small table that isn't in its usual spot. I don't have time to think about these details, though, because the clock is already telling me it's six-fifteen. *I have to hurry*, I think anxiously. It's only when I start to move my chest that the memory of yesterday storms back. My ribs are imprisoned in a steel vise and my heart is inside out. I'm not in my room and my pain isn't from sore muscles. I wasn't having a nightmare.

Leaning on my forearms, I drag myself out of bed with Sash's help. I've never hurt so much in my whole life. Even when I fell off the wall at school and had to have thirty-three stitches, I didn't suffer this much. I feel like a thousand vultures are devouring my rib cage.

Sasha holds out a pen and paper.

"Is your pain more this way or that way?" she says, pointing to the two extremities of a line going from "No Pain" to "Unbearable Pain."

I laugh in spite of myself, and a burning sensation perforates my abdomen. Anyone else would have just asked straight out, in a quivering voice, how much it hurt. But not her, and it comforts me.

"I'm fine," I say, pushing aside her paper and pen.

"Liar," Sasha whispers, serious.

"What about you? Did you manage to sleep a bit on your own?"

"Like a log!" she lies. Her swollen lids and red eyes betray a sleepless night.

"Don't worry, I'll sleep with you tonight. We'll figure

something out," I tell her, taking her trembling chin in my fingers.

She looks at me and I know she doesn't believe it any more than I do.

"If we call Mom right away, she'll be here by the end of the day," she says, her eyes brimming with hope. "She could even come get us at school instead of him."

He, the stranger, shakes my thoughts, which are now clear. We can't do what Sasha's suggesting. He'd use that phone call as another example of my supposed teenage crisis. He'd make up something. He's already done it before, once when I asked Erika if I could stay at the library until eight o'clock to study. He convinced her to say no, telling her I wouldn't use the time wisely and Sash would be influenced by my bad example. She believed him. She always believes him.

My word is worth nothing against his.

Maybe he's even called her already. The stranger is as sneaky as he is dangerous. If we have to tell Erika, we can't do it by phone.

"We'll wait until she gets back," I reply.

"But Phoenix, she's not back for another month! By then, you–"

"Promise me you won't tell anyone until then," I say.

She shakes her head no. Her feet are restless.

"Please, Sasha, for me!"

She thinks, looking out at the lake. A tiny "I promise" filters out through her lips. I hug her and whisper that she shouldn't worry. What happened yesterday is past, it won't happen again. I tell that to myself too, but I'm not convinced.

The stranger doesn't speak to me. He drives without taking his eyes off the road. It's like I no longer exist to him, while he's never been more present in my mind than he is today. Even from the back seat, I sense his tiniest movements—scratching the tip of his nose, drumming his fingers on the steering wheel. I'm on my guard.

Once we're stopped in the school parking lot, he turns around suddenly and I jump. He notices and pulls back a little, his back pressing into the steering wheel and honking the horn. Beside me, Sash stifles a cry, her hands over her mouth. A few people turn and look at the car, including Dean, who flashes me a smile I don't have the strength to return. The teacher waves at his students.

"Your mother and I have decided you won't go to drama club anymore," he says to Sasha, sounding like a journalist reading from a teleprompter.

"So you told Mom *everything*?" Sasha dares to ask, the news about drama club not even affecting her.

I put a hand on her restless knee. She doesn't seem to notice. All her anger is focused on him.

"Some things should stay between us, for the good of our family," he explains, staring at her.

Sash swallows loudly, feeling for my hand.

"Do you understand what I said?" he asks, threateningly.

I nod, unable to breathe.

"Sasha?"

"Yes," she murmurs.

The car doors open, but the world as we know it closes up and disappears.

TWENTY

I've never missed Dad so much.

I'm almost sure I've cried out for him every night since I've been sleeping alone. If you can call it sleeping, because without Sash, I barely sleep, and when I do, I'm plagued with nightmares.

I dread the night almost as much as I dread the stranger. I wake up in a sweat around four in the morning: a poisonous terror infects my heart, which feels like it's two beats away from stopping. Unable to go back to sleep, I cling to the memory of Dad like a life preserver. In his last postcard he promised that soon he'd send us an address where we could write him. Sasha pointed out that he could just call us, and she's right. But this minuscule hope is all I have left. To be honest, I'd a hundred times rather write to him than talk to Erika. She thinks I lie as easily as I breathe. But Dad would believe me and come back as quickly as he left. *You have a debt now. A debt to those with your name*, as an author we both love wrote. It's true, he has a debt to write us, to call us. He has to do it, has to come home.

Who except Dad can I talk to about the silence of the night? Our mother has picked her side, and the shadows under Sasha's eyes are already too deep. Our father is the only person who could handle what I have to say. He'd remember how much I love falling asleep to the sound of Sash's voice. It would be intolerable to him that I have to do without it. I'd tell him about my new bed, where I'm suffocating like a fish out of water, counting the hours until morning. I'd whisper that some mornings, I wake up disappointed that I haven't dissolved into the night itself.

I know the situation hasn't changed. Five thousand, one hundred, and twenty miles separate us from him. He doesn't call, he can't hear us, and I'm forced to keep quiet. Nothing has changed, and yet everything is different here, for us. From the outside, it's impossible to notice any disruption. The stranger has become careful. He spares my face so no one will see the bruises. I just have to change carefully into my gym clothes, wear big sweaters, and stay in the shadows. Nothing I'm not used to.

We wear the same clothes. Clouds are still white. The leaves are still dead. Our voices sound the same. But if you looked a little closer you'd realize that the wind is blowing the wrong way, my bruises are endlessly refreshed, and we've never looked more tired. We could collapse in slumber in the middle of the hall, our legs drifting from under us like sand. Sasha often falls asleep in the car on the way home from school, sometimes even a few inches from her plate at dinner. I'm different. I stay awake. One thing is for sure: we're no longer moving forward. We meander like two ghosts, with vaporous steps and sunken eyes, between two worlds: their world— the world of the Baldinis, of Vanilla, of Dean—and ours.

At first, I tried to act like things were normal. I summed up *Legends of the Fall* by Jim Harrison for Vanilla, telling her to watch the movie with Julia Ormond so she could impress Dean. I explained to Bertie about Sasha having to drop drama club, pretending we had too many things to do at home. I smiled at my teachers, nodded along to Vanilla's monologues, participated in math and history class. That lasted a week and a half. For those ten days I carefully avoided Marlon. He was different: I couldn't look into his eyes and pretend that everything was fine. Not after what he told me.

When he spots me, his face lights up like he's seen a divine apparition. I don't get up off the bench to hide in the restroom, as I've gotten in the habit of doing. I tell myself it's time to face him. I've decided to put an end to our friendship—no matter what we've become to each other.

If I can't tell him the important things, I won't tell him anything at all.

I know our conversation will be hard and that at some point he'll storm off—the end. Sasha calls that "our parents' disease." The automatic departure, leaving as the solution. I've seen Marlon operate this way many times, especially with girls when the discussion isn't going the way he likes. He loses his cool, crashes into something or someone, then calms down in the nurse's office.

Once I'm on Marlon's blacklist, I'll become invisible again.

"Are you avoiding me because of what I told you?" he accuses, without saying hello.

"No. Definitely no," I protest weakly. He's got it so wrong that I'd scream at him if we weren't in school right now. But I can't raise my voice so close to the teachers' lounge. I can always feel the red dot from the sight of a rifle on my forehead.

"Why, then? Because honestly, I've racked my brain,

I don't understand what I did wrong," he insists, raising his voice.

"Not here," I whisper.

He sits on the bench, concerned, furtively watching me. *Not here* makes no sense to him.

"Where, then? My place?" he asks, smiling, his face leaning over me.

I pull back bluntly, staring at him icily.

"No, I won't go anywhere with you. I'm already seeing someone."

Right away I regret having said that.

We stay side by side like a proton and electron, two particles with opposite charges. After a few minutes, the tension becomes unbearable. Marlon is the first to propel himself from the atom, standing, looming large above me. I feel myself folding like a collapsible telescope.

"Well, I'm going out to smoke. See you around," he says, emotionless.

I clutch the little notebook in my pocket as I watch him walk away, counting each step. I keep counting for a long time after he vanishes from my field of vision. But the numbers have no more meaning.

He doesn't come back. Not that day, or the next, or the next.

I was distraught, desperate even, when I made the mistake of confiding in Vanilla. I made her swear not to say anything but she did even worse than that. She published it on her blog. PHOENIX REJECTS MARLON. WHO CAN CONSOLE THE DEVASTATED PLAYBOY? "Freedom of information," she explained, pointing to the photo of Marlon—eyes closed, head in his hands— probably taken after a losing swim meet. His defeated look has nothing to do with me. I've seen him in a very good mood, laughing, several times since our altercation.

But over the next few days, a dozen anonymous, insulting notes wind up in my locker, accusing me of breaking up the golden couple—Annabelle and Marlon— over the summer. Insults are scrawled in marker on the doors of every toilet in the building. The stranger gets wind of it, of course, and I suffer.

As if the situation isn't complicated enough as it is, this morning he's the one helping me erase the graffiti. "Rule number one, DISCRETION!" he explodes, certain of being alone with me. "But no, you can't even manage to respect that!" I don't even listen to his interminable reproaches, knowing full well that the worst is yet to come.

When I finally manage to corner Vanilla, who's been avoiding me like I'm a leper for a week, she explains that no one wanted to be seen with Brutus after he assassinated Caesar.

"I'm not Brutus," I say drily.

"No, but Marlon is more beloved than Caesar."

I observe her reflection in the mirror for a long time. That's when I notice a new expression, like a boss about to fire a sick employee.

"Are you serious?" I say. "*You're* going to ditch *me* for this?"

"Just until things calm down," she begs, smiling innocently.

"It's fine, I get it." My voice is suddenly so loud that Vanilla turns red, ashamed. Rightly so, since she's the one responsible for my shaming. If she hadn't published that junk, I would have managed to make myself smaller than the tiniest elementary particle.

The message is as clear as can be. She'll say a quick hello if she passes me in the halls but there's no way she'll support me. The blog post I might have expected from her—but not this. Which makes it even more painful to digest. I can't believe she's pushing me away at the very moment I've realized how much I need her by my side. She was my last defense against the stranger, my tiny act of resistance. I could say, "See, I'm talking to

Vanilla even if you forbid it. You can't touch me there."

"Sorry," she says, shrugging her shoulders.

"It doesn't matter. Don't count on me anymore for your synopses."

Ever since, I'm alone.

TWENTY-ONE

They say the month of November snatches the last leaf
from its branch. Here, the trees have been bare for over
a month. It's cold the way only dreary little towns know
how to be cold, the skies swirling with snowstorms and
the main street abandoned as soon as the last shop
closes.

Sash thinks that nature *knows* and is having
her revenge. That it's the wicked stepfather's fault
that November feels like January. She interprets
changes in the weather like a fortune teller reading
palms—it's some quackery Dad taught her. But if the
weather has so much power, I ask myself, why hasn't
lightning struck the stranger? Why hasn't he been
carried away by an unexplained hurricane or a tsunami
at the edge of the lake? If the universe is so merciful,

why hasn't the stranger joined the Norwegian yet?

Anyway, I don't believe in that stuff anymore. If a bitter chill and an early freeze is nature's best plan of action against Smith, I'd rather stick with science. The stranger won't be defeated by a cold.

In front of Sasha's school, gangs of pompom-hatted heads flit and giggle. She doesn't play with them. She never runs around anymore after school. She's sitting on a bench across the road, staring at the edge of an icy puddle and tapping it with the toe of her boot.

"The trees are so scrawny!" she cries when she spots me. "Did you know last winter they cut down acres of forest because the ice froze the sap and cracked the trunks? Do you think their sap keeps them warm enough, or are they cold like us?"

"You can ask them. In the meantime, they aren't lucky to have a scarf, like you, so please put yours on right," I say kindly.

She puts her arm around my waist, pointing with her mitten to a giant poplar with hornlike branches.

"He looks even sadder than you," she says, serious.

"That's because he hasn't gotten his four-thirty kiss yet either."

I'd rather keep things light. I don't want to spend my precious alone time with my sister talking about what's eating away at us. She laughs, and her kisses rain down on my face like a meteor shower.

"You know, I can never be sad when I'm with you. Never," I say, looking her in the eyes.

I hope she never doubts that.

She smiles at me shyly and wraps her scarf around her neck. We sink into the mud of the football field to head to the high school parking lot.

On the way, Sash nibbles on her snack, examining the bark of each tree like she's a forest ranger.

"Don't rush or anything," we hear the stranger shout from where he's parked, a short distance away.

Sash, startled, drops her juice box, spilling it all over herself. Through the open car window, he looks furious, his face as red as a maple leaf. I quickly wipe the grape juice off her coat. We know what a grave sin it is to soil the leather in his car.

He gestures for us to get in, and fast. We obey. We don't think about orders anymore, we act. We know very well what a slow response will cost me.

"Your mother came back earlier," he tells us, irritably.

I think he hates surprises almost as much as he hates me. I smile at Sash, who looks small behind her huge schoolbag, holding it on her knees like it's a shield. Her face lights up. This means we'll have a little relief.

"Why are you smiling?" he asks her, his eyes in the rearview mirror.

"It's me, I made her laugh," I shoot back.

"You think I'm an idiot?"

No, not an idiot. That's not the word for him.

He starts whistling along to Tchaikovsky's "Waltz of the Flowers," his long fingers miming the conductor's baton. Bertie's van comes back to my mind, and listening to Cat Stevens with the Baldinis ... I'd trade a weekend with Erika to spend just an hour in their company.

The stranger turns off the ignition but doesn't get out. We don't move either.

"If, by some mysterious chance, your mother is given any reason for concern in the slightest, I will send Phoenix away to boarding school and Sasha will stay here with me," he breathes. His eyes are closed, as if he is talking to himself.

Sash opens the door suddenly and vomits. I feel like doing the same. Vomiting to show him how much he disgusts me. Only I'd do it inside his precious car, all over his leather seats and his respectable gray coat.

"I think I'm sick," Sasha mumbles.

Her forehead is beaded with sweat and her eyes are glassy. I help her into the house wordlessly. I'm afraid if I open my mouth I'll scream, and I don't want to add a panic attack to whatever bug Sasha's caught. After sitting her down in the front entrance, ignoring Erika, I dash straight back outside. I have to get out as fast as possible or I'll crack. Any slip of the tongue could mean boarding school.

The stranger mutters something inaudible, handing me our things from the car.

"*Boarding school.* You understand me?" he repeats, his face an inch from mine.

I nod, leaning back. He gives me a quick push, then steps away. I think I could strangle him with my bare hands. I could grab his neck and squeeze with all my might.

I don't follow him back inside. The house isn't big enough to contain my hatred. I run to the mailbox desperately, like an animal being hunted down. My mind feels like a Tetris game gone wrong. Thoughts pile upon each other in a jumble. Numbers and equations no longer make sense. It's all a disaster, I think.

Between piles of flyers, I spot a Venezuelan stamp on an apple-green envelope. I rip it open, thinking only about Dad's address.

My big and little asters,

The river I'm looking at now reminds me of our lake in autumn. I hope you're taking care. The address I promised you is only a few thousand miles away. In the meantime, I love you both from the north the east the west and the south of my heart.

Your Dad

My hand is on my chest, for fear my heart will fall out. I read it again. I recognize the last sentence—it's by André Breton, another absent father. He also wrote to his daughter, hoping she'd forget being mad at him. I don't know if it worked on her, but for me, what we had is broken. Too many things have happened and there's no way out now.

That damn address, I needed it today!

I turn back, chilled to the bone and as dry as a twig about to snap.

After she drinks a cup of warm milk with lots of honey and reads the postcard, Sash falls asleep, her husky throat purring. I sit in the half-light beside her, remembering my childhood nightlight that projected stars on the ceiling. *Count the clouds in the sky / Count* *the centipede's legs / Count the beats of my heart / Count till you're not afraid.* I whisper our rhyme over and over when the sound of the telephone rings out from the first floor. She's sleeping too soundly to hear it. I close the door behind me, letting her enjoy a rare moment of rest.

I sneak out to listen to the stranger on the phone. I sit on the stairs at the top of the landing, out of his sight, my ears pricked.

He speaks calmly.

"No, like I told you already, she doesn't want to speak to you ... I'm sorry ... Thanks, you too ... see you on Monday."

He hangs up and mimes putting a revolver to his temple.

"Who was that?" Erika asks.

I'd bet our biggest beetle, the *Goliathus goliatus*, it was Vanilla. She and I are the only ones who can inspire such contempt in him.

"Marlon Baldini," he says, rolling his eyes.

He speaks the name with such scorn that I almost think I've heard something else. If it was really Marlon, I hope nothing has happened to his parents or to Bertha. After the way I treated him, Marlon wouldn't call me if it wasn't important.

"I thought she wasn't seeing the Baldinis anymore," Erika says, surprised.

"She isn't, but obviously the poor kid hasn't got the message," he replies, mockingly.

They laugh, and that laugh goes directly into the pantheon of the ugliest sounds in history.

Erika starts to come upstairs, and before I have the chance to slip away she's in front of me, smiling. She sits on the step beside me, but we're not on the same side. I stop myself from telling her that she shouldn't be here, that she belongs on the stranger's team now. We stare at the splinters along the baseboards, not speaking. There's as much warmth between us as between two random people sitting next to each other on the train.

"You have an admirer," she says.

I've got nothing. We're not going to talk about boys, especially not Marlon. We've never done it, and we probably never will. Anyway, today is not the day for gossip.

"When are you coming back?" I ask, changing the topic.

"I haven't even left," she remarks softly.

I won't let myself be swayed by her mother-hen voice. Just because she's in a good mood, it doesn't mean I can trust her. Her visits are as ephemeral as a glass of water in the desert.

"When?" I insist.

"I'll be back before Christmas," she finally says.

Another month without water. Alone with him. I feign apathy, though it feels like a hailstorm of anvils is driving me into the center of the earth.

"So long?" I barely manage to speak.

"Our most important clients always make decisions at the end of the year."

"Mmmh," I murmur, standing up.

"I'll miss you," she says, hoping I'll sit back down.

I freeze. I know how much that must have cost her to admit, but her absence costs me much more every day. She has no idea how hard my armor is. I climb the stairs without turning back. In all honesty, the only reason we miss her is because the stranger keeps his fists in his pockets when she's home. Nothing more than that.

Her pale eyes burn into my back until I close the door of my new room behind me. There's a gulf between us, an immense gulf of the long months we've spent in hell with the stranger. And as long as he lives in this gulf, we can't build anything between us.

The rest of the weekend passes slowly and without incident. One more act in the play that's become our life.

Sasha—suffering from the flu—spends her days sleeping, like she's trying to catch up after the insomnia of the last few months, or else save up for the days to come. Meanwhile, the stranger, Erika, and I watch television, wrapped under the same blanket in front of the same boring movie. I'd have happily buried myself elsewhere, in some complicated equations, or watching Sash, but the stranger insists on spending the afternoon with Erika and me. "For me," he begs, putting on a theatrical pout. My only outlet for revenge is thinking of them with fierce hatred. I imagine them disappearing underground, sucked down by a vengeful goddess, a spirit of the forest.

There's no one worse than these two people, in my opinion.

Afterward, we walk outside, talking about my prospects at St. Joseph's Academy. My future—not conditional—prospects.

"A hundred miles outside of town, there's a school dating from the nineteenth century, a little Neo-Gothic jewel with brilliant teachers, at your level of intelligence," the stranger recites in the manner of a tour guide.

I trip when I hear "a hundred miles."

"The chemistry lab is impressive," Erika adds.

Of course. They've already visited.

"And tell her about the library!" he adds, pointing to me.

It's immense, she says, with a ladder to reach the books up high. A film collection, private rooms, two hundred acres of oak trees, an astrophysics program, specialized courses—everything I've dreamed of since birth is to be found, according to them, at St. Joseph's Academy. "Everything you love," Erika assures me. Except that *everything I love* is currently sleeping in our house, I want to protest.

Without Sasha, they might as well just send me to the gulag; it couldn't feel any worse.

Enrollment in boarding school isn't a threat, like the stranger made me believe. It's as real as a broken rib. The application has been accepted, my bed reserved. He's managed to convince my mother to send me after the holidays. They've come to the agreement that Sash and I need to be separated so that we can reach our full potential. "You're suffocating each other and it's not healthy," Erika says, as if she were talking about an all-vegetable diet. I can't even care about the details of where and why. All I can think of is that one sentence: *I will send Phoenix away to boarding school and Sasha will stay here with me.*

Who will protect my little sister if I'm not here?

TWENTY-TWO

"**Oh great, just what I needed!**" the stranger fumes, looking at the truck from the sawmill through the living room curtains.

It's his order of wood for the fireplace, arriving earlier than expected.

"Clean yourself up, and not a word!" he orders, referring to the bloody nose he's just given me. Usually he's careful not to leave visible evidence, but this time he was too angry. I take the stairs three at a time, stick two cotton balls in my nostrils, and put on a clean sweatshirt.

Sasha is stationed in front of the bedroom window, smiling like it's Christmas Eve. When she sees me, she startles and her mouth tightens shut, but she makes no comment. "Don't say anything and it won't be real,"

I've repeated endlessly, making her promise to close her eyes when it gets bad. I'm not proud of teaching her to ignore reality. But if she can't see what happens, she has nothing to hide.

"Look, they're here!" she exclaims.

I join her, and immediately understand what it must have felt like to be in Roswell in 1947, discovering a UFO on your ranch. Two flying saucers are heading toward our front door. Ivan and Marlon.

I hear them talking to the stranger.

"Sasha! Phoenix! Come say hello!" he shouts gaily.

We rush out to the landing.

"I hope you haven't come to pick up your essay, because the girls haven't given me a spare minute to get marking done," the stranger is joking.

Marlon laughs, intimidated and polite, until he spots me coming down the stairs. All of a sudden, he looks like a cartoon character with a black storm cloud above his head.

"Hey, strangers!" Ivan cries, arms held wide.

Sash throws herself at him with her full weight. They embrace, for so long I start to think I'll have to pull her away. I know her tears are like a jack-in-the-box, ready to spring out at the least hint of kindness. But thankfully, I don't have to intervene; she moves away on her own, looking down so that no emotion shows. I pull her toward me, greeting Ivan with a nod. Marlon raises his hand, distant too.

"What did you do to yourself?" the stranger suddenly asks, squinting at my face.

He couldn't care less about me. He was the one who just messed up my nose.

He holds out his hand and I take a step back. The pain hits my sinuses, as if I had just snorted gravel.

"I'm just bleeding a little," I answer belatedly. Talking to him in public is hard, not least because Ivan and Marlon are looking at me as if *I'm* the impostor. I can't manage to concentrate.

"Do you want to have a hot drink or some food before you hit the road?" the stranger asks them politely.

"No thanks, we'd like to get home before the roads are totally buried in snow," Ivan replies distractedly, rubbing his scar, his good eye staring at my nose.

I smile at him. I get lost in thought, imagining that after this they'll join Prudence for dinner. They'll eat without sarcastic comments, without teeth chattering against the silverware, without fear. It sounds like paradise. Marlon follows the men outside to unload the wood when Ivan catches his shoulder with a quarter-back's grip. They exchange a few words, but their voices are too low for us to catch the frequency.

The stranger gestures to me and Sasha to stay inside, though my scarf is already around my neck.

After Marlon comes back inside, the three of us stand in the hall like statues.

"Can you show me the box with your super-cool beetle?" he asks Sash.

She drags him upstairs excitedly to her room, what used to be our room. I still haven't had the courage to move my things to the new room, apart from my blanket and pillow.

He freezes on the threshold, as if there were a log blocking his path into the room. Clumsily, he takes off his hiking boots and his big jacket covered in just-melted snowflakes, dropping them in a heap in the hall. I start to pick them up but he protests, putting his hand on my arm. I pull away violently and his boots hit the ground with a thud. I start to shiver with fear, then relax when I remember that the stranger is outside the house. Marlon gives me a puzzled look, possibly searching for the old Phoenix, the one who didn't startle at the slightest gesture or sound.

"You can't leave without seeing the beetle with the yellow mandibles that Phoenix found this summer, when she was looking for you!" Sasha commands. "It's

162

a specimen from the *Nicrophorus* family. That means they–"

"Bury carcasses to feed their young. I've done my research," he cuts her off, shyly.

He leans against the closed door, his arms crossed, waiting for my sister to finish rummaging through the bell jars and insect cases. I sit down at the desk with my back to him. I don't want him to get the wrong idea; he can't stay here.

"You should sleep at night," he says, accusingly. "You look like a zombie. A pretty zombie, but still."

I don't turn around. There's no room left in me for compliments. There's no room for anything.

"Zombies don't sleep, they're dead," Sasha points out.

I tune out as they debate the many degrees of death of zombies, werewolves, and other supernatural beings. Then, suddenly, Marlon stops talking and walks toward me, crouching next to my chair. He's spotted it, on the desk in front of me: his broken box. I open my mouth to explain, then reconsider. Even though I really want to, I can't tell him I'm sorry.

He looks at me like I really have turned into a zombie, or maybe some kind of replicant, an alien being he has no hope of understanding. I pretend not to notice and grab the first book that materializes on the desk: *Analysis of Differential Equations.* The series of mathematical formulas lets me pretend I'm nothing more than a bunch of *x*'s and theorems in an abstract realm—elsewhere.

The wooden floor creaks a few inches from my foot. Through my painful, blocked-up nose, I smell chlorine.

"Are you going to keep acting like this?" Marlon says, his voice full of contained rage. "You lied. You're not going out with anyone—I asked Vanilla. If you knew the courage it took me to ..."

He doesn't finish his sentence. It gets stuck somewhere, the place where all important words hide.

My lips cemented shut, I grab a piece of paper and a pen. But my zigzagging parentheses and shaky *y*'s reveal my unease. Marlon stands up suddenly and shuts my book.

I jump.

"For fuck's sake, what's wrong?" he shouts, impatient.

Here we are.

"Do you speak Norwegian?" Sasha suddenly asks, coming to the rescue.

"What? Uh ... yeah, a little," he says in a dull voice, surprised by the question.

I recognize that miserable look on his face. It's the same one I must have whenever I hear students put the name "Mr. Smith" next to a description like "really cool teacher."

"Say something," Sash orders.

I stare at her, hoping she'll change her tack. *Norwegian* is not an innocuous subject.

"Please," she adds, thinking she hasn't been polite enough.

Marlon massages his chin, looking perturbed. He's speechless. Sasha takes his hand and makes him sit on her bed, then, without warning, wraps her arms around him. She's smart enough to understand that she's touched a nerve with this subject. He holds her close, his face buried in her curls.

I realize how alike the three of us are. We carry something dead deep inside us, something nothing and no one can ever bring back to life.

I decide to intervene.

Usually, Sasha and I imitate Spanish and Swedish accents, but Norwegian can't be too hard to make up.

"You could speak Norwegian to him," I suggest. Marlon smiles at me as if I were the solution to a complicated problem.

I look away. I had forgotten how much he means to me. I spent months admiring him in secret, hoping one day he'd end up in my room smiling at me this way, happy, maybe on the verge of kissing me. I imagined the scene thousands of times, thinking of his fingertips wrinkled by water, wondering if you could feel the hours spent in the swimming pool when you touched them. I never would have imagined wanting to show him out the door as soon as possible, being unable to look at him. But if he stays any longer, I'm going to make a mistake. I've had the truth on the tip of my tongue for days now, the intense desire to tell everything to anyone, it doesn't matter who. *It doesn't matter who* can't be Marlon.

"*Graïtufluctu daïlikilu? Flaïglutu?*" Sasha says, giggling.

He explodes with laughter, and it's like a carnival breaking out in the middle of a cemetery.

"*Jeg tror jeg elsker deg,*" he says suddenly, very softly. His voice is different and the sounds seem odd. Maybe he's mocking us, making words up too. But something in the sadness of his look tells me that this phrase has a special significance.

"What does it mean?" Sasha asks, still holding Marlon tightly in her arms.

"Look it up," he replies, in a voice close to a whisper.

We hear a long whistle from outside. It's different from the wicked stepfather's, which is as ear-splitting as a foghorn.

"I have to go," Marlon says.

Ivan's signal, then.

We accompany Marlon to the front entrance, not saying a word. He drops a kiss on Sash's forehead, and she tells him to give Prudence a hug from us.

"And you, say hi to me at school, at least on Fridays," he implores me.

I turn my head toward the crackling fireplace, closing my eyes. When I reopen them, the door is closed and the motor of Ivan's truck is making the windows buzz.

I flutter my eyelids, finding it hard to adjust to the emptiness in the house.

"When you're finished daydreaming, I need help stacking the wood correctly," the stranger snaps at me. "That cyclops is incompetent."

I assent, on guard again.

It's true, I *was* dreaming. I dreamed of Marlon and Ivan, of our life before, of the thousands of feelings jostling around in me when I'm near them. But I have to wake up. For our good and theirs, I can't let the stranger tarnish the Baldinis too. We have to know they're safe, invincible. It's my duty to keep us away from them, to keep their kindness unsullied in the deepest part of our hearts.

TWENTY-THREE

I hurry to pick up the phone in case it's the stranger again. He's out at a school meeting he couldn't avoid. He calls every half hour to check that we haven't escaped, knowing it would be impossible for us to get anywhere in less than thirty minutes. Under the thick, powdery carpet of white out there you can't even tell the ground from the frozen lake, as if the world were nothing but an arctic desert. The snow never stops falling, in thick, creamy layers like a Napoleon pastry. It's out of the question to venture anywhere. Our tracks, and probably Sasha herself, would get swallowed up, erased.

To my great surprise, it's not him. I hear a woman's nasally voice; a Doctor Gould, from a hospital in Maine, wishes to speak to Mr. Jessup Smith. She speaks to me kindly, asks if I'm his daughter, and without leaving me a chance to reply, adds that her call is of the highest importance. The receiver slides from my hands, they're so sweaty. If I hang up on her, the stranger will find out and he'll be murderous. But if I decide to be the messenger, I'll have to face him and repeat whatever private information this doctor is about to tell me. Either way, I'm in trouble. She insists, so I agree to take the message. She announces that my "grandfather," Jeremiah Smith, has suffered a serious hemorrhage caused by cirrhosis of the liver. Right now he's in intensive care in critical condition. "I must emphasize the *critical*," she says. Finally, she tells me to inform my "father" as soon as our conversation is through. I write her number on my arm before hanging up.

I'm shocked to realize that the probable death of someone close to the stranger doesn't sadden me at all. I've raised the battlements so high between myself and the world that no feeling can reach me.

"Cirrhosis is a chronic liver disease," Sasha recites, recalling a definition from memory. "It's an alcoholic's disease. You think his dad is one?"

"I don't know."

"You think that's why we've never seen him drink?"

"I don't know, Sash," I say wearily.

Despite my silence, she keeps talking about this

strange telephone call, trying to clear some of the fog around Smith—the man from before the violence, the one who still deserves a name. Jeremiah Smith might explain the mystery around their family, the absence of photos and keepsakes, the stranger's refusal to talk to us in any way about his trip out East. It would explain the holidays spent in Maine, the strict, hard childhood, the sacrifice of his studies in medicine, and his profound hatred of hospitals.

"All we know is that his father is dying," I conclude.

"You're right. Nothing makes what he does to you okay," she says.

I nod wordlessly. Talking about our *situation* always makes me feel like I've undergone electroshock.

I try to reach the stranger, but he doesn't answer his phone.

Sash suggests I leave him a voice message or a note on his desk so I don't have to tell him in person. But his reaction to that would be even worse. She insists on staying with me, but I don't sway. I never sway anymore. I'd rather sit in the kitchen and wait for him after I make sure my sister is asleep.

"Why do you have to suffer everything all alone?" she asks me sorrowfully.

I turn out the light. It's easier to reply in the

darkness, where I can't make out her expression.

"Because I can," I say solemnly.

"I've had enough of you being a hero!" she says, bursting into tears. "We have to talk to someone, Phoenix. To Ivan or Prudence. She's a nurse, she'll know what to do."

I wipe away her tears of rage, stroking her cheek. I can't even begin to picture her solution, because I don't have a speck of courage left in me. I'm not a hero. I never have been.

All I can picture is running away. But we have nowhere to go—where would we stay?

And that's not what's important. Sasha's panic attacks have gotten worse. Maybe because now they're being triggered by a cause much more serious than the death of a baby bird. They're rage attacks. Even scientific theorems no longer work as an antidote. She's become impervious to Einstein, Galileo, and all the rest.

Despite my efforts, Sash simmers, her rage barely below the surface. Some nights I almost don't recognize her. Her eyes brim with such rebellion that it could make an armed regiment flee in terror. I'm afraid one day the walls will break and a flood will escape, at the wrong time, in the wrong place.

"If you need to tell someone, tell the trees," I whisper gently.

"I might as well tell Erika, for all the good that will do! I want to tell it to someone who will believe us, who will do something!" she shouts.

An affectionate sigh escapes me. I don't have the heart to fight anymore.

Silence descends.

Sash pulls the covers up over her head. I kiss her hair where it sticks out from under the blanket and I tell her, "Don't still be mad at me tomorrow, okay? Because I'll always love you more than one more day." My words sound useless, even to me, but they're all I have left to give.

TWENTY-FOUR

The next evening, the stranger went to the airport to fly to his father's bedside in Maine. Before he left, he took care to leave me some souvenirs, which I've spent all weekend putting ice on. He also called Erika to tell her about his trip, but she can't come back to "watch" us because she has a difficult contract to negotiate.

So for three days Sash and I have been alone. But the prune-colored stain under my eye has been attracting the attention of my schoolmates.

I'm walking with my head down, my knit cap pulled down to my eyebrows, when something strikes my shoulder. I feel pain rousing in me. He's come back early. My eyes close and my throat constricts as I wait for the hiss of an insult.

"It's you," says Marlon, delighted.

I gaze at him for a moment, not knowing what to do. He smiles at me, looking amused. I keep walking at full speed. It's four thirty-two, two minutes late. Right now I have a clock in place of my brain, a constant, oppressive *tick, tick*. If the stranger isn't here, he might be waiting for me at the front door or in the kitchen, counting down the minutes to my punishment.

"You in a hurry?" Marlon asks, following me with long strides.

"Yes."

"If you have to take the bus because Mr. Smith isn't here, my mom could drive you home," he suggests. "She's picking me up in fifteen minutes."

That "Mr. Smith" pierces my eardrums even though Marlon's voice is full of care.

"No thanks," I reply, flatly.

He smiles and escorts me outside, pulling up the collar on his jacket to protect himself from the brutal wind. I get the feeling he won't leave before we reach Sash's school.

"Is it because I'm not part of your gang?" he asks, pointing at my eye.

"My what?"

"Your shiner. It's not the first," he observes. "If you don't belong to a gang, I have good reason to be worried, right?"

I don't react, and he doesn't press the matter. Still, beneath my layers of wool sweaters, the stone walls around my heart are shaking. I know that I should be panicked that Marlon is on the trail of the truth. But just the fact of knowing that he still worries about the state of my face gives me such a feeling of warmth that the atmosphere seems different, as if all of a sudden I'm in the shade of a weeping willow on a hot summer day.

Marlon walks carefully on the patches of black ice strewn across the sloping road. He skids with each step and I find myself obligated to hold him up, one hand constantly on alert at his back. When my fingers meet his, boys wearing parkas in the school swim team colors whistle inanely at us.

"You should get a proper pair of hiking boots," I suggest. "With crampons."

He opens his eyes wide, and his smile is so big that I feel like I'm a miracle, a mute who's rediscovered her voice.

"I really miss this," he says, his legs still unsteady.

The puff of vapor escaping from his mouth seems very thin compared to the strength of those four words. I step away from him. I have the feeling that's all I do, distance myself. Soon I'll distance myself so much I'll disappear.

"I miss *you*," he specifies, facing me.

I miss him too, but I've missed everything for a while now. It's like Sash and I are living in a faraway country, with an impenetrable border separating us from the people we love.

"The bus will be here any minute," I say.

It's already four-forty. What's Sasha doing? The bus comes at ten to. Marlon takes a cigarette out of his pocket and leans against the same tree as me.

"I can help you, you know. Whatever's happened, you can trust me," he says. "You don't have to explain."

He's not joking. I can see it in his pupils, which look like two little blackbirds stuck in the snow. I can feel tears creeping across my eyelashes.

"Oh, Marlon!" Sash cries at just the right time. "I'm so glad to see you! We were thinking about you this morning, right, Phoenix?"

Unfortunately it's already four forty-eight; there's no more time for reminiscing.

"We can't be late," I say, pulling Sasha by her arm.

Marlon waits until we're sitting on the bus to go back up the hill, his steps faltering. I have an intense desire to get off the bus and run after him, but I don't have the right.

I thought naïvely that the absence of the stranger would give us a bit of peace, but I was wrong. We don't know when he'll be back, because he refused to tell us and we haven't spoken to Erika. So we're always on guard. We go home immediately after school for fear that he's waiting for us at the bus stop, not far from our house. We do our homework fastidiously, being extra careful, not forgetting even a comma. We do our errands with his lists branded into our skulls. We worry that he'll check the garbage cans or detect an unusual smell. "In a horror film, you die because you underestimate the monstrosity of monsters," Sash says.

The saddest thing is seeing Sasha going to her room at night, alone, even though we'd been planning to sleep together like before. I thought I could make my sister forget what's divided us by sharing some happy moments again. But the stranger has seeped into every corner and nook of our existence, like a specter. He haunts us, and that's even more nerve-wracking than seeing him here in the flesh.

The fear is so extreme that sometimes we see his shadow at night in a shirt falling off a hanger. Being afraid of a shadow: I can't think of anything more pitiful.

TWENTY-FIVE

Today, Sasha refuses to go with me to the greenhouse. "Why—to see what's left of the flowers?" she asks. She has a point. Only two orchids have attempted to endure the winter. The other plants died of cold three weeks ago. Still, those two survivors remind me too much of me and Sasha to abandon them to the frost: the way they hang from their cracked stems, their petals in a void, looking like shipwrecked castaways. So I care for those two orchids as if our lives, too, depended on it. We're strangely connected to them, like Elliott is connected to E.T.; one suffers when the other's in pain.

I wonder what will happen to us when the greenhouse is nothing more than a graveyard.

I don't linger outside because the wind is so sharp it feels like it's biting my bones. Its gusts carry fog, denser than a block of iridium, making it impossible to see the house from the edge of the garden. I quickly choose four large logs from the woodpile, then all of a sudden I hear Sash scream. I run, dropping the wood, slipping on patches of black ice, my boots sinking into the pile of snow around the porch.

Inside, my sister is hopping up and down, overexcited. I pull off my coat like it's stopping me from breathing.

"Are you crazy?" I cry, out of breath. "Do you know what I thought?"

"He sent us an email!" she shouts, throwing herself at me.

Before I can comprehend, she grabs my hand, pulling me to the living room.

Our email inbox is up on the computer screen.

From: isidorcotton@gmail.com
Subject: It's Dad!
To: phoenixandsasha@gmail.com

My big and little beetle,
Here is my address: isidorcotton@gmail.com
I won't leave the village of Celestún until I hear from you.

Tell me everything I've missed!

Dad

P.S. I caught an azure *Lycaenidae* the color of your eyes, Phoenix. I hope I can give it to you soon.

I sink into the chair and read the message again. *There's what you call a twist in the plot.* Sasha grabs the mouse and clicks on "Reply," hopping up and down with impatience.

"What are you doing?"

"What do you think?" she says, giggling.

"What are you going to write him?"

"Everything," she says distractedly, fingers on the keyboard.

I push her aside with my shoulder and close the windows in three clicks.

"He's waited almost a year and a half to ask for our news. He can wait one more night."

Honestly, it doesn't matter to me whether we write him today or tomorrow. I have a handful of banalities I can tell him, and Sash has as many anecdotes as her memory can hold. But I reject our father's assumption that he has the right to our trust. He lost that the day he left us, like you'd leave your suitcase in a checkroom at a hotel. Except that the suitcase is lucky. You walk around empty-handed for a bit, then go back to pick it up—a few hours, maybe even a day or two later. You don't wait more than a year before realizing you're traveling abnormally light. You don't worry how it's doing seventeen months too late, when it's already damaged, destroyed.

Sasha was right. An absent father is not a dad.

"I want to write him!" she exclaims. "You can't stop me."

We look at each other, our eyes battling, our fingers on the keyboard. I pull back abruptly. What's happening to us? We aren't enemies. Obviously she has the right to email Dad. If it makes her happy.

"Just be careful not to tell him everything, okay?" I remind her gently.

"Yes, I understand," she assures me, patting my head.

I'd like to make her promise, but I don't want to start a fight. If she says she understands, I shouldn't doubt her.

"You want me to stay to turn out the lights?"

"No. I'm not scared anymore," she says. There's a strength in her voice that I'd have a hard time finding in myself. Maybe my bravery was always an endangered creature and the stranger has made it extinct once and for all.

Sash pulls me toward her and kisses me. I know I

wasn't kind with her. I slide my fingers through her curls and press my forehead against hers. Her breath is warm on my nose.

"Feel how much I love you!" she says, laughing, her mouth opening wide, breathing on my face.

How will I survive without her, at boarding school?

"Don't worry. If I hear the car, I'll call you," she reassures me.

Then she motions to me to go upstairs.

You'd think our roles had been reversed, that she's the one whose job it is to comfort me now. That the car she's talking about is not the stranger's, but something cheerful, like the pink ice cream truck that comes around in the summer.

Like a little girl, I go upstairs to finish my homework, letting Sasha take care of the adult business in the living room.

TWENTY-SIX

A sound echoes through the house. Maybe the faraway echo of a siren. No, more like an alarm clock, getting closer and closer. I open my eyes: it's ten after six. Saturday morning. There's no reason for the alarm to be set.

Suddenly, I realize it's the telephone ringing. My body sleepy, I hurtle downstairs and grab the receiver.

"Hello," I say, trying to sound alert.

"Phoenix?"

It's one of those moments when gravity disappears, your feet leave the ground, and oxygen feels scarce. I don't have to search my memory to recognize the voice.

"Dad?" I mumble, breathless.

"I woke you up, Phoenix. You sound like one of Sasha the Muchacha's zombies." He laughs and I hold the telephone away from my ear, closing my eyes to stop the tears from flowing. When I open them, the Muchacha is standing there in the middle of the living room, hands over her mouth.

What did she write him that he would call so early, so soon?

"Are you there? I don't hear you," he says, worried.

Am I here?

I nod my head before emitting a sound like the wheeze of an injured animal.

"Listen to me, beetle. I know I'm the last person you want to talk to. I don't have a lesson for you. You've been braver than a Masai warrior. But it's enough, okay? You've had enough for a lifetime. So you're not going to think, you're just going to do what I say. You call Ivan the minute you hang up. You tell him to come get you, that it's an emergency, that there's a fire, a wolf, whatever. If he doesn't pick up, I want you to get yourselves out of the house as quickly as possible. You hear me? You go to Bertha's, to the bakery, wherever you want. You. GET. OUT."

I can't. I've already thought about it.

Fear and stress flow through my veins like venom.

"And ... and then?" I stammer.

"Then, I'll probably already be there."

That's not what I mean! I want to scream. I mean the

stranger. Who knows what he's capable of? If he runs away, like a coward, we'll live in fear forever that he'll find us again. There's a flaw in every escape plan. Unlike Dad, I've had the time to think through every possibility, one dead end after another.

"You don't have a choice, Phoenix, you—"

I put my hand over the receiver to block Dad's words. I hear tires squealing on the road. It must be him; no lost drivers ever come this way.

"He's here," I whisper, as if the stranger could hear me.

"Give me Ivan's number!" Dad orders.

I pull Sasha by her pajama sleeve and climb the stairs frantically, two at a time, forcing her to keep up with me.

I find the business card in Marlon's box and read the numbers to Dad in a clear voice.

"It'll be over soon," he promises before hanging up.

I quickly put the phone down.

Sash shivers in the doorway of her room. Her toes are blue with cold and her eyes red with tears. I wish I could tell her that I forgive her, that it's better this way, that she's done well, anything so she stops looking at me as if we're about to die. Only I don't have time. "What are you waiting for? Put on some socks and get back in bed, quick!" I say sharply.

185

The car engine has already been switched off.

As soon as my head hits the pillow I listen for noises below. The keys are thrust into the lock, a bag falls to the floor, shoes squeak in the hall. Once the coat is unzipped, I hear the coffee maker sputtering out steam. I don't dare swallow, much less think about the call from Dad, for fear of missing an important sound.

He climbs the stairs, then places his cup down on the bedside table, puts his toiletries back in the bathroom, opens the closet and closes it again. I've learned to familiarize myself with the stranger's routines. After the racket of slammed drawers is over, silence descends on the house, punctuated by the *tick-tock* of the clocks. Sasha coughs here and there. Wind rushes into the air ducts, whistling like a pressure cooker.

Time passes and stretches, a Möbius strip where you can't find the beginning or the end.

Sash shakes me like I'm a snow globe.

"Wake up. Ivan and Prudence just rang the doorbell," she whispers.

How did I manage to fall asleep?

I get up and dress calmly. I avoid stepping on the floorboards that creak and I don't say a word. Through the window, I can see that the deep-blue sky is still tinged with darkness. I look at the clock, which reads seven.

Numbers, I think, *concentrate on the numbers*. I'm trying to be as rational as possible because if I let myself get taken away by emotion, Sash will get it in her head that our ordeal is over. And when we have to shut the door on hope again, she'll be inconsolable.

We descend the stairs slowly, stopping on the last step, facing the front door. The Baldinis look serious under the porch light. Shadows hide the top halves of their faces, like war paint. Still they're both beautiful, a beauty so pure it fills my heart.

"To what do we owe this early-morning visit?" the stranger asks, sounding concerned.

Prudence and Ivan ignore his outstretched hand. A gust of wind sends pages of a notebook on the apothecary chest flying. I try to breathe through my mouth since my nostrils are blocked. They're full of the stranger, of the suspicion and aggression that emanates from him.

"We just want to talk to the kids for two minutes," Ivan replies, his jaw clenched. He takes a step forward and his weight makes the floor creak at the hall entrance.

"At seven in the morning? What for? What did they do?" the stranger asks impatiently.

I would so much like to tell him to shut up, but I can't do it. I can't put the fear aside. I've forgotten everything else. I don't know anymore how to oppose him. Paralyzed,

I watch Sasha, who's gnawing on her nails. She won't speak without my permission. She promised.

Ivan sighs loudly, passing his gloved hand over his molten forehead. His magic scar is correct. It's in front of an abominable being.

"Get dressed, sweeties, we're going for a drive," Prudence says lightly.

With his back to us, the stranger straightens, like a wolf ready to jump. He glances at us. We step back.

"What is this farce?" he says, stunned. His voice is firm.

Sasha hides behind me, terrified. Her panting breath burns my spine. Ivan advances, forcing Smith to back up against the wall to let him past.

"Help the kids get their things," he tells Prudence, not taking his good eye off the stranger.

She comes in without hesitation, wiping her shoes on the doormat as if this were a friendly visit. She even takes the time to hug us.

"Just grab the essentials," she says, looking at us with care in her eyes.

I'm not sure what she means by "essential." Out of instinct, Dad's hunting rifle comes to mind. Loaded with two cartridges. Its butt wedged in my armpit, my index finger on the trigger, the muzzle on the forehead of ...

"Look at me, Phoenix. Breathe. Everything is okay.

Your boots are all you need."

~~I glance to where the rifle is hidden,~~ underneath
a board, just a few feet from Sash. Her hands are
trembling, making me think of a field of poppies before a
storm. I help her tie her laces, trying to hurry. Suddenly,
I look over at our coats. They're behind the door he's
leaning on. I can't confront him, not unarmed.

"You won't need them. It's warm in the house,"
Prudence assures me.

"In the house," I repeat, as if she were speaking a
foreign language.

We let ourselves be led, still worried. Ivan moves like
a magnet, shifting at every instant the wolf tries to hold
us back.

"What is it you think? You can't do this! I'm going to
call Erika!" He sounds like a spoiled child.

"It's already done, goddammit!" Ivan growls, his fist
hitting the door.

My sister and I gasp, then we freeze, heads down,
afraid of being turned to stone if we accidentally look the
stranger in the eye.

"Come on, girls!" Prudence exclaims, putting her
arms around our shoulders.

We walk as fast as we can on fevered legs, not turning
around, all the way to Ivan's truck.

My mind is a blank. It's been two hundred and forty seconds—exactly four minutes, I counted—that we've been sitting in the car in silence, watching the porch, when we hear a rough cry. Prudence locks the car doors and grabs the wheel. Her knees are moving restlessly but her face is calm. Maybe she's lived through a scene like this before, with Marlon's dad. I wonder if she knows how it's going to end, or if she's just like Sasha and me, unable to predict what will happen next.

Sitting close to Sash, I put my hands over her ears to block out the sounds of breaking objects coming from the house. I need her to stay calm. "Close your eyes," I tell her. She obeys. She doesn't see the stranger coming out of the house like a shot, his nose bleeding, followed by Ivan, walking calmly, hands in his pockets. Neither of them speaks, as if this were a silent film—in red and white. The stranger stops in front of the truck's headlights, blinded. We're backlit, invisible to him, but it's a strange spectacle to see him helpless, hunted, his body faltering in the snow. I bury Sasha's face in my chest. She can't open her eyes to this, whatever happens. She's already seen enough.

Ivan stands still as the stranger goes to the dock and jumps with both feet together on the ice.

"Where is he going?" Prudence asks.

"Onto the lake," I reply.

At these words, she unzips her parka, relieved. I notice her striped pajamas. She smiles at me, running her fingers through her tangled curls, embarrassed that she's not more put together. If I could speak, I'd tell her there is no woman in the world more beautiful than her in this instant.

Our eyes meet and an unbreakable connection forms. Because she didn't take the time to groom, to dress, to understand the details. It was enough for her to know that a man—someone thousands of miles away, someone she doesn't even know—asked her to get in the car at dawn to come help us.

She believes us and that's worth all the families in the world.

The stranger disappears at the edge of the lake, a silhouette in the fog. Ivan turns back with the expression of a hunter coming home empty-handed. He climbs into the truck and takes the wheel. Prudence slides over next to me, but doesn't touch me.

She's right. I need space to absorb what's just happened.

TWENTY-SEVEN

Sasha and I are in shock. We're not thirsty, or hungry, or cold, or hot, as we try to answer the umpteenth police officer asking how we are.

If we were going to break down, we definitely wouldn't do it surrounded by strangers and drunks, slumping listlessly on plastic chairs that grate loudly at the slightest movement. In any case, we're not going to shed one tear for Jessup Smith. We've sworn it to ourselves.

It was three days ago that he ran out onto the lake and no one was able to find him. We didn't feel safe anywhere. Ivan shut himself away with us, his rifle resting on his heavy thighs. Huddled against him, we barely spoke and he didn't try to make us.

Then, this morning, the police called us to come down

to the station. "The divers found his body a few miles from your house, under a large beech tree," an officer explained.

Maybe our beech, the one we jump from into the lake in the summer. Mother Nature got her revenge after all. Sasha was right. She was on our side from the start. The signs were there; I was just too full of despair to see them.

Erika comes back from the morgue, where she identified the body. She dabs at her eyelashes to stop her mascara from running. She looks heartbroken and it makes me feel sick. Briskly, she pulls herself together, doing a U-turn and disappearing behind the wall covered in missing person notices. I hear her busying herself; coins clink, some roll on the floor. She reappears after several minutes, her eyes red but dry, two steaming cups in her hands.

"Careful, it's hot. You hungry?" she asks. "I can get you something from the vending machine if—"

"Can we go back to Ivan's?" Sash interrupts. It's the first thing she's said all morning.

Erika and Dad study us, timidly. I think they're too ashamed to refuse or even to give us permission, as if they've deprived themselves of the right to be our parents. They seem to wait for my signal, trusting me with the important decisions. Even though all I want is to rely on them. Still, I assent with a nod, too exhausted to get into complicated discussions.

"We should tell Prudence," I say.

"Yes, of course," they say together.

They go into action. One hand in a pocket looking for car keys, cellphone to the ear. *Where's the exit? This way. Where are you parked? That way.* Heads bump, legs run into each other, nervous laughter. We watch them gravitate around us like two servants, eager and docile. *You didn't forget your hats? We could have a bite at Archie's? Or get something to go? You always like their omelets, right? And bacon?* We don't know what to reply; we can barely remember the last question. They're so disoriented it's making us dizzy. They're anxious, full of remorse, terrified of making a new mistake. Dad most of all.

You should have seen him when he got here yesterday. I don't know how many times he apologized before collapsing in our arms. He wept a long time, then made a point of honor of "telling us everything," straight away. After all the months of silence, his words came out with a strange ease, as if he were reciting a poem, like he'd done for us so many times before. Except that this poem I didn't particularly like.

The truth is that he abandoned us for a stupid

sabotage mission in the Falkland Islands. He was offered a second chance by the Earth Liberation Front after the failure at the slaughterhouse, and, blinded by his ideals and dreams of adventure, he said yes. He didn't think about the consequences. And when—"after several miles"—he realized what he had done, "it was too late," he admitted. I didn't want to hear any more and I told him that. He opened his mouth but I shook my head. "It's not that it's too late, Dad," I said. "It's too soon." And it is. For me, anyway. It's too soon to go back to what we were. Forgiving him right now is more than I can handle.

We get to the Baldinis' house, but I don't want to go inside. I want to see the white valley marred by that hole in the ice, to convince myself that Jessup Smith is really dead.

Except for Prudence, I don't think anyone knows how to ask us questions about what happened. They're afraid of our answers, afraid they'll be too upsetting. When I do tell the truth, it won't be to get anyone's pity, or to horrify people with tales of the wicked stepfather.

I'll tell my story so I can mourn this fearful, silent Phoenix. So I can leave a few flowers at her feet and let her rest forever, lifeless, deep inside me.

But right now, I can't do it yet.

Suddenly Prudence is at my side, her shoulder touching mine.

"It's a habit you have to break," she says.

"What?"

"Thinking he's always behind you," she says, obviously recalling her own fears.

She's right, and knowing she's right makes my heart tighten. Each time someone cleans their glasses, I remember the terror.

"Every dark-haired man will always look like him from the back," she continues. "Which is lucky for you."

"Why's that?" I ask, hurt. I can't see any luck in this story.

"Because you like blonds," she teases.

I laugh, embarrassed. There's one I like, yes.

"Come on, come inside where it's warm. There are no more wolves, no monsters, no ghosts here," she says.

TWENTY-EIGHT

Today, Sasha is thirteen years old and has a boyfriend who keeps her too busy to talk to me on the phone some nights. But she's still obsessed with zombies. With her theater troupe, she dresses up and terrorizes the town. The new town.

We couldn't find a way to rebuild ourselves in the place where we'd been broken. We were going around in circles in that house haunted by the past, unable to project ourselves into the future. We needed a new place, one where we could find ourselves again. Sash seems happy here. If she's not, at least she fakes it well, since her panic attacks are rare now. "It's the warm air and the flowers," Dad says. He's still a sailor at heart. He bought an old houseboat, which he lives on, but now it's moored for good, not far down the lake from Erika's new house. I don't know if I've totally forgiven either of them for leaving us, but they haven't given me any new reasons to doubt them. We try to spend every Sunday together, the four of us. And if I forget, our mother is the one who calls and urges me to join them as soon as I can.

Sure, there's still the "vortex effect," which Joan Didion described so well—all those unexpected triggers that pull you into the whirlwind of remembering. It could be a child crying at the bend of the road, a window slamming shut, an alarm that's too near. Almost anything; almost everything. But there it is, the solution to the problem, in that hopeful *almost*.

Prudence was right. I've gotten used to not looking for the wolf in a crowd, not panicking when someone taps my shoulder to ask the time. I still startle, but fear—real fear—I've unlearned it. It's been replaced by the harmless kind. Being afraid of a pigeon pooping on my new coat, for example, is a cheap, ordinary fear that I love more than anything.

Of course, the past would bother me a lot more if I didn't live with Marlon.

We enrolled at the same university so we could watch over each other. It's like our hearts are at each end of a seesaw, balancing each other, keeping us level.

But we share an apartment as two old friends, nothing more.

He doesn't talk about girls, but I know girls talk about him, as he's lost none of his charm. When he gets out of his theater classes, I hear all the pretty actresses commenting admiringly. Some of them think I'm his sister when they see us walking side by side, and he doesn't correct them. He winks at them and taps the tip of my nose as if I were Sasha. They giggle and I hate them all. In my entomology class, when someone asks me about him, I pretend I don't know him well, that we're just roommates. But I'm not an idiot. Every Friday night he goes out, with a cigarette hanging from his mouth, and at dawn I stand on the threshold to his room, looking at his empty bed. Angry at him for choosing Friday—*our* day—to leave and forget about me, taking away all the meaning it had.

Sometimes it hurts so much that I have to leave the apartment. I can't stand being in that space where I feel him even when he's gone, with the plants he brought home for me, the clothes on the drying rack with his chlorine smell, the drawings he slides under my door when he thinks I'm angry but I'm just jealous, and all the other little things that connect us invisibly.

Obviously, it's too late to tell Marlon there's no one for me except him. I had my chance and I let it slip away.

Last night, Sasha called me and said, "It's time." We don't need many words to understand each other. *It's time to go back*, she meant. To go into the past again and set fire to it, like Erika did with Dad's things.

Marlon drives us, not asking questions, picking up Ivan and Prudence on the way. So we'll have backup in case one of us drowns in emotion and Marlon can't console us on his own.

The thing that strikes me the most is how the house hasn't changed. I was expecting it would be swallowed up by time, but it's still standing, looking just as it did that night in December. I think of the theater, where the set decorations change to show time passing. In reality, it's the people who change.

The land around the house is wild now, hard to access. Reeds and wildflowers grow above the porch, through the floorboards, taking back their rightful place.

I walk around the house, inhaling the summer: muggy and flourishing, the way I love it. Insects buzz around the flowers, forming a cover on the garden. I venture in, parting the long stems of asters, treading on the dry and cracked earth. I don't dare set foot in the greenhouse, which looks like a jungle, teeming with life and brambles.

Sasha gives me a hug before going off with the Baldinis and Pan, just like she used to. She wants to see if our beech tree is still there.

"Do you want to be alone?" Marlon asks.

"No. No, you can stay."

We're sitting on the dock. Suddenly, I feel the weight of everything I want to tell him in the pit of my stomach, like a sack of stones. If we decided to go for a swim, I'd drown.

"You remember the box I made for you?" he asks, timidly.

"Of course, yes. I still have it. I use it to collect the pens you're always leaving lying around," I joke, trying to give myself courage.

He laughs softly and I realize he's still the same boy from Fridays at school. My heart beats faster in the July heat.

"*Jeg tror jeg elsker deg*, do you remember that too?" he asks solemnly, looking to the opposite shore.

A woman shouting from a paddleboat makes me turn my head. I wait for the vortex to pass before replying.

"I remember, but you never told me what it meant."

"You never looked it up," he says, accusing.

Because I wasn't sure it was something important.

It would be easier to live in a comic book. We wouldn't need to be brave. We'd have sentences there, all ready, above our heads.

"You don't want to translate it for me because you're not sure if it's still true, right?" I say, defiant.

He turns to look at me sharply, as if I've just spit on him. I have tears in my eyes. I move my foot a little in the lake to splash him, trying to make him smile. But he shakes his head, maybe trying to clear it of the words he was about to say. He stands up and heads toward the car. I feel like I'm reliving that time I told him I was going out with another boy, and it pierces my stomach. I don't want to make the same mistake again. I have no more reason to lie to him. I run up behind him and grab his hand. He pulls away, putting his arms up.

"*I think I love you!* That's what you couldn't be bothered to look up for five fucking years! That wasn't so complicated, right? I THINK I LOVE YOU!" he shouts.

I shake my head then move toward him, not knowing what to make of his anger. I've seen it directed at teachers, politicians, bad movies, but never at me.

And that declaration? What is it worth after all this time?

"You're not saying anything. As usual," he says

calmly, looking disappointed. "You've never said anything."

"That's not fair, Marlon. I do what I can with what I have left," I confess sadly.

Then he laughs, a bright shard ricocheting off the surface of the water.

"We're arguing when it should be the best day of our lives," he finally says.

I'm too shaken to reply.

I stay quiet for fear of saying what I shouldn't. Yet again. It's totally stupid, obviously. I have thousands of words for him inside me, piled up over the years. I need time to excavate them, but I feel time running out.

He shrugs his shoulders and kicks at an anthill. He looks like a little boy whose friends have all gone on vacation without telling him, leaving him alone and bored all summer.

I still have this stupid cork in my throat.

"Even Fridays, you let me leave like you don't even give a damn," he accuses. "I have to go sleep at Dean's or everything reminds me—"

"Come over here, or else I can't do it," I interrupt.

He lifts his head and walks straight toward me.

"I don't think I love you," I murmur, looking at his knitted eyebrows. "I'm absolutely sure of it."

Our faces are inches apart. Marlon puts his hands on

each side of my neck and leans down, and the whirlwinds calm in the distance. *Each kiss a heart-quake*, Lord Byron wrote. An accumulation of energy that's suddenly unleashed, creating deep fractures in the earth. But this time he's wrong. Nothing can be fractured; everything already is. Instead, this kiss is the first pillar of a building, finally rising from the ground after years of planning and work.

Prudence whistles, then applauds. They join us almost immediately.

"Phoenix, you're supposed to look for beetles on the ground, not in this guy's mouth," Ivan teases.

We laugh, forgetting the house, the lake, and all the awful memories.

Marlon takes my hand and I smile at Sasha, a smile that's the first of many more.

Nastasia Rugani was born in 1987 in a very small town in France. Half-Croatian, half-Algerian, she grew up in a multicultural environment where everyone had a funny story to tell. As a child she enjoyed wandering around with boys, skating, and playing with mud and insects.

After graduating, Nastasia entered the famous Sorbonne University to become a journalist, but quickly realized she was too shy. When she discovered Maurice Sendak, Kitty Crowther, and Robert Cormier, she decided she wanted to write children's literature, and completed her first novel while finishing her bachelor's degree. Full of fear, she sent it to her favorite publisher, and they sent back a very enthusiastic letter. She spent months rewriting her story, and became a published author at the age of twenty-four. Since then she has written two more novels, including *About Phoenix*.